The Glory of God Saved My Life!

STEVE SMITH

ACKNOWLEDGEMENTS

I am eternally grateful unto God for all his many blessing. God has been better to me than I deserve, and His goodness has given me an attitude of gratitude. I want to first of all dedicate this book to my wife Rita, with whom I just celebrated twenty-five years of marriage. She has been a God send, a true definition of what a Proverbs 31 Woman is. She left her job to be by my side, and has accompanied me on every doctor visit without hesitation or complaining. Between Emory Hospital (Atlanta), UAB (Birmingham), and Gadsden Regional, I was admitted into the hospital eight times in one year.

From the time I first got sick in February of 2013, she has never left my side. Through all the doctor visits, hospital after hospital stays, praying to find treatments for this very rare blood disease called ITP. She has been the epitome of a wife and mother, and most of all her calling as an intercessor. While the devil was trying to kill me, at the most weakest point in my life, he forgot that I was married to an intercessor. We've been blessed with three beautiful children, LaTasha, Steven, and Jamaica. God did it, of course, and I give him all the Glory, and all the praise, but I'm truly blessed to be married to a woman of God who knows how to get in touch with Jesus!

Secondly, I dedicate this book to my grandbaby, "Shekinah." God blessed us with the most beautiful grandbaby in June of 2013. It was right in the middle of our troubles when she was born. She wakes up with the most beautiful smile on her face. She brightens the room when she's in it; she calls me "Poppie."

At a time in my life, when I was facing the worst storms I have ever had to endure, she brought a joy to my life that was unexplainable. I mean literally, like, I had to undergo heart surgery in May, SHEKINAH was born in June. I want to thank God for bringing her into our lives at the time when I needed her most.

Thirdly, I want to dedicate this book to the beloved members of New Destiny. I have always known how blessed I was to pastor such a wonderful congregation, but it was during this storm in my life when I saw what the church was truly made of. I was already teaching on the "Glory" when I was diagnosed with Thrombocytopenia, (ITP), but when I was hospitalized the very first time, the church began to demonstrate what they had been receiving for months. They began to petition God for an atmosphere of his

Glory. They also established a 5:00 a.m. Glory prayer call, praying for their pastor four days out of every week. And they still do it to this day.

Without prayer, we can do nothing. I am so happy to have been chosen by God to suffer for Christ's sake. "And he said unto me, My grace is sufficient for thee: For my strength is made perfect in weakness. Most gladly, therefore, will I rather glory in my infirmities, that the power of Christ may rest upon me. Therefore I take pleasure in infirmities, in reproaches, in necessities, in persecutions, in distresses for Christ's sake: for when I am weak, then am I strong" (King James Version, 2 Corinthians 12:9-10).

Finally, I am thankful to my loving caring family, who prayed without ceasing. Even when my condition went from bad to worse, my family was there. I am eternally grateful for my parents, James F. Smith and Estella Hendricks, and Earl and Anna Heard; you have been a God send.

God has favored us with two beautiful angels, who are now a part of that great cloud of witnesses in glory, our grandmothers, the late Mrs. Charlotte Brookins, and Mrs. Shirley (Muah) Thomas. Both helped to shape my life; they are now in heaven. Thank you God for allowing my life to be touched by theirs.

Every person needs to have someone in their lives to whom they are accountable. I am blessed to have many friends, both near and far. I am eternally grateful to be surrounded by so many wonderful people, many of them are pastors. But there are a couple of guys that my wife will call when things around the house start getting crazy, and I would call these guys at 3:00 a.m. in the morning if need be. Thanks for all you do: Stacey Brooks, Minister Ocie Hope, and Bishop Dexter Elston.

I also want to thank my Hematologist, Dr. Umo Borate, (treated ITP blood disease); the Medical team at UAB Kirkland Clinic, Birmingham, AL,; Chief Thoracic Surgeon, Dr. Daniel Miller (performed my heart surgery) and his staff at Emory Hospital, Atlanta, GA.; my primary care physician, Dr. H.B. Thompson, Gadsden, AL.; and Dr. Alan Pernick, Gadsden, AL.; last, but certainly not least, I would like to thank my pastor, Dr. R. A. and Lady Victory Vernon of The "Word Church", Cleveland, OH. Thank you for always praying for us, calling and checking on us, speaking a "Word of Hope" when I was at my lowest point. Thank you for releasing that word into my life, and reminding me that "There's a miracle in my mouth". We are thankful to be a part of the greatest fellowship in the world, "The Shepherds Connection", under the leadership of Dr. R.A. Vernon.

TABLE OF CONTENTS

INTRODUCTION

What if God came to you and told you that He had a plan for your life? Probably you would be quite excited to receive news like this. Better still if God told you that he was going to do great work through you. But great work requires preparation and few of us are truly ready to be agents of God without working on ourselves and perhaps even going through some trying experiences as God works on us.

The focus of this book is my experience of God working through me and an account of my experiences being worked on and eventually working for God on the plan he developed for me.

I will say, too, that I am more in awe of God now than I have ever been in my life. Although I've suffered a great deal in the last few years, as God developed his plan for me, I have become a stronger and better person – a better helper and follower of God than I could have been before.

In 2013, God removed the hedge, and allowed the adversary to have access to me. The only reason Satan was able to test Job the way he did was that God had removed the hedge and had given Satan access to Job; He allowed Job to be tested. "Hast not thou made an hedge about him, and about his house, and about all that he hath on every side? thou hast blessed the work of his hands, and his substance is increased in the land" (Job 1:10).

As God removed the hedge from my life in 2013, I went through a period of trials and tribulations from which only God could finally deliver me. I faced cancer, blood platelet transfusion, bone marrow issues, heart surgery, chemo and also staph infection. I was hospitalized numerous times and I also faced death during that time of testing as I fought for my life. In the end God received all the "GLORY", and He alone is worthy to be praised. In reality, the devil thought that I would be dead by now, my story is one that I hope will help answer the question we all have heard over and over again. "Where are the miracles that we read about in the Bible?" The answer is simple, they are found in the GLORY. If you ever want to see what a miracle looks like, take a look at me. It is a hard thing to wrap my mind around and realize even now. But through all that I have endured, fearful though I may have been at times, I have still had a praise inside me, and today I am still able to give God the "GLORY" for all the things He has done!

1

WHAT IS THE GLORY OF GOD, THOUGH?

The word Glory is found many, many times throughout scripture, in both the Old and the New Testament. And what it represents is something incredible, something amazing. I personally believe we all use the word too casually in our daily lives. We have all heard the saying, "whenever purpose is unknown, then abuse is inevitable." For if we really understood the magnitude of this word Glory, we would also know that when the Glory of God is present, the "atmosphere of heaven" is then also present, which means the barrier which once separated heaven and earth has now been removed. That means anything can happen for you, when properly aligned with the word of God. This being said, if the barriers which separate heaven and earth are removed, then heaven and earth have now become one and the same. This is why Jesus said, in the Model prayer, "thy Kingdom come, thy will be done, in earth, as it is in heaven." Jesus literally taught his disciples to pray for the will of God to be done in such a way that they would not be able to differentiate between heaven and earth in terms of their experiences. He advocated, in a way, that his disciples should be able to access the realm where things are present but still invisible – an idea that I will talk about more in a later chapter.

GLORY IN THE HEBREW IS (KABOWD)

The word Glory in the Hebrew language or Old Testament appears as "kabowd" but what does this mean? Well, in Hebrew, the word "kabowd" literally meant weight. Although it was also often used figuratively to denote splendor, honor, or abundance of some kind. As stated in Guillermo Maldonado's book "The Glory of God", he says that in the Old Testament in particular, the word also serves to describe a person's wealth, power, majesty, influence, or honor. Kabowd is also an expression of God's Glory and can refer to a revelation of God's divine nature.

GLORY IN THE GREEK IS (DOXA)

Now that we've looked at the Hebrew word for Glory, let's also take a look at the Greek word, because we see Glory mentioned in both the Old and New Testaments.

When the Pentateuch, the first five books of the Old Testament, first appeared in Greek, the word "doxa" served to describe God's Glory and appeared the closest thing to the word "kabowd". In terms of its meaning, it served to denote the majesty of God, as well. The Doxa is a form of God's Glory that is also an aspect of God's nature.

THE SHEKINAH GLORY

The Shekinah Glory, however, is the visible, tangible, manifestation of the presence of God as it appears to mankind. The Shekinah Glory differs from the other two forms we have discussed because it transcends the spiritual realm to affect the natural realm. The Shekinah Glory refers as well to the immediate activity of God and also tends to reveal the presence of God in action. In my experience, people are far less likely to refer to this particular aspect of God's glory.

JESUS IS THE BRIGHTNESS OF GOD'S GLORY

The Bible refers to Jesus as the expressed image of God. But as we go through definitions of God's Glory and other such concepts, let's be clear about exactly what this idea of the expressed image actually means.

First, Jesus is the highest level of the manifestation of God's Glory. If anyone ever wants to know what to look for when looking for the Glory of God, all you have to do is look to the life of Jesus.

Jesus established the atmosphere of heaven in every situation. By doing this, he also compelled things and people around Him to change for the better. There was no choice but for things to improve. But what do the Scriptures say precisely about Jesus in this sense?

In Hebrews 1:1-3, we have: "God, who at various times and in various ways spoke in time past to the fathers appointed heir of all things, through whom also He made the worlds; who BEING THE BRIGHTNESS OF HIS GLORY, AND THE EXPRESS IMAGE OF HIS PERSON, and upholding all the things by the word of his power, when he had by Himself purged our sins, and sat down at the right hand of the majesty on high."

In layman's term, to put this in a way where even the babes in Christ can understand it, the Glory Of God is simply the " spiritual weight of God". And I can only speak from personal experience, I believe that the full magnitude of God's Glory will not be realized as described in Habakkuk 2:14, unless you are willing to pay the price.

What price? Well, if you are reading my book it is because God has stirred you and for whatever reason, your hunger has intensified. Whatever has compelled you to pick up this book and make a decision to read it, it is something profound.

GOD WANTS TO THROW HIS "WEIGHT" AROUND

Let me start by saying that the God we read about in the Holy Bible is the same God we serve today. The Jesus that we read about in Scripture is the same Jesus we serve and represent today.

We see that the same Holy Spirit, leading Paul in Acts 16, being lied to in Acts 5, and speaking and separating Paul and Barnabus in Acts 13, is the same Holy Spirit that dwells in us today. For some strange reason we have a tendency to think that we serve a whole separate trinity from the one we see operating in the Bible. We see God, Jesus, and Holy Ghost in the Bible but disassociate ourselves from them in our lives.

We have been programmed and taught not to expect God to enter into our lives. Personally, I see this as one of the obstacles. We are told that God will not necessarily be available to heal, deliver, set free, and perform miracles. But God is looking for people who will partner with Him in the earth. He wants to align with people who will not only see things as they are, that are right in front of them, but people who will perceive things beyond themselves – understanding, too, the scope of God's Glory.

The Glory of God is the weightiness of God. His Glory is literally about "throwing his weight around" and existing within the atmosphere of heaven. For us to fully realize it, we must also try to recognize all of the barriers between heaven and earth. We must perceive them and remove them.

In Isaiah 60, the word of God says "Arise and shine, for thy light has come, and the Glory of the Lord has risen upon thee". It is not that the Glory is not available , but we, the church many times fail to recognize the Glory, and more importantly, the purpose of the Glory.

The Glory of God is literally the environment of heaven. To make more sense of this, the air is the environment of earth, but the Glory is the environment of heaven. Come Sunday, hundreds of thousands of people get up every Sunday morning, get dressed, attend church, sing, dance and shout, but never experience the Glory. I do not believe that God would have us to just show up on Sundays and Wednesdays and never see the miracles of the Bible taking place in our local church.

But what changes have we really made? What sacrifices have we made for the Lord to advance the Kingdom? What are we willing to give up to experience the Glory of God on a deep and intimate level?

Not long ago, I was moving through my life, giving sermons, speaking about things that inspire me; moving without much real sense of direction. Then, suddenly, I discovered that God was up to something much bigger than I could ever imagine. In fact, He was about to take me on a journey that I could not prepare for and He was about to show me some things in the Spirit that would not only change me, but also our congregation.

What began as a routine quickly became a revival and began to break out beyond our church as well. I have literally been stuck in the Glory to this date – going back to the New Year. And, yes, while you may be wondering what happened for the Glory to show up in the first place, for it to have any impact on my life at all, when, to varying degrees, it is so special, understand that several things had to happen for God to show up in the way that He did and for Him to manifest His desires as he did.

First, there must be a hunger and a passion for the Glory of God. I have come to a place in my life now that I can no longer do ministry without the Glory. Glory is necessary for me to go on preaching the word of God, not because I lack faith but because I know the power of the Glory. I know that the Church, without the manifestation of the Glory, will not have eternal value.

THERE MUST BE KNOWLEDGE OF THE GLORY

Second, there must be an awareness of the Glory. Habakkuk 2:14 says, "the whole earth shall be filled with the knowledge of the Glory of God". We all need the knowledge of the Glory because there is no lack of Glory. We can fail to recognize it, but there is no lack of it.

Yet, most Christians will never realize the Glory of God. Even though they go to church, they go through the motions of faith, they have not had an encounter with the living God. They have thus not experienced what is necessary to spark the type of fire of which I am speaking.

This passion has nothing to do with your salvation – you love your God. You are saved. You are going to heaven when you die. This is the case if you believe. But the Glory of God allows us to have something, to do something more. We can experience the environment of heaven while living on Earth. Your entire life can change through the joy in Glory and the hope in Glory, too. Anything is possible when you embrace this phenomenon.

GET PEOPLE TO THE GLORY

Knowing what I know now, I will never see ministry the same way again. I will never perform ministry, either, as I said, without the Glory of God. Since then I have come to realize that it is absolutely possible, to create the right environment for a miracle.

Fish need no instruction once they find themselves in water. This is because water is the right environment for them. An eagle doesn't need instructions once he finds the open air. Once he finds it, it becomes his environment. It is the same for believers. Believers still need to be convinced that the Glory is where they belong. They need to be convinced it is their domain; the place where miracles are the norm.

In January 2013, I set out to accomplish one thing – to get people to the Glory! How is this to be done? Well, it first has to be done over a period of time. It was not something I expected to accomplish in a single sermon or in a single week of sermons.

I have learned a great deal from my Pastor, Dr. R.A. Vernon of the "Word Church", about how to preach in a series, and honestly, I have found this method of preaching in a series, over a period of time as probably the most effective method for encouraging people to follow the Lord; to persuade people to allow the Lord to lead them.

I also keep in mind that God did not recreate the universe in one day, or one hour. He could have, if He wanted to. But instead he decided to extend creation over a period of six days. He then decided to rest on the seventh day to even take stock of his creation and enjoy it. Some things simply cannot and should not be rushed. The message on the GLORY, for it to really be effective, could not be rushed. Because we have been very methodical to slowly teach this series on GLORY, it has literally transformed our Church.

As I write this book, I have to admit that I have not preached a sermon in a whole month, due to my recent diagnosis of a rare blood disease, known as ITP (Idiopathic Thrombocytopenic Purpura). But because our people were already in the GLORY before I succumbed to my illness, my illness had had little impact. Teaching the GLORY, rather, has catapulted our ministry. I have seen our Church grow both spiritually and naturally, with leaps and bounds, because people are in the GLORY and they were brought into the GLORY over a period of time, through consistent discussion and focus on the GLORY.

You may be saying as you read this book that you are already in the GLORY, too. But before you make that declaration, before you really allow yourself to be convinced of that and perhaps even think about laying this book aside, allow me to ask you a few things:

- Have you stressed the importance of the GLORY to yourself and others recently?
- Have you intentionally sought after the GLORY?
- Has the GLORY of God been revealed to you personally?
- Have you created an atmosphere of GLORY conducive for miracles?
- Have you reached the level of faith where you believe what the Bible says?

2

THE GLORY OF GOD SAVED MY LIFE

In January of 2013, I began to see bruises showing up on my lower body. I would wake up and see a bruise on one leg, but I would not think much of it, because I assumed because of the of work I do, I had bumped into something which caused a bruised. Then a week later, another bruise would show up on the other leg, but again, there was no pain associated with it.

I was a very sick man, walking around, like a walking time bomb. I was not even aware that I could have dropped dead at any time, because of my condition. I had a very rare blood disease known as Idiopathic Thrombocytopenic Purpura (ITP). It was so rare, that the doctor I was seeing at that time, had never treated a patient with this disease. ITP is an autoimmune disease, which there is no known cause, and for which there is no cure. It can only be treated. Because I had no pain associated with all these bruises, I discounted them as nothing. I was one fall away from being dead.

I want to put a peg right here, because we as men have a tendency to deal with pride, and also a spirit of stubbornness. While I thought I was doing the right thing by not communicating with my wife, I did not know that the enemy was trying to kill me. And the longer I went without telling my wife Rita about the unexplained bruises, little did I know my health was failing me.

In the meantime, the unexplained bruises were not only on my lower body, they were now showing up on my arms and chest, back, and eventually these bruises where all over me, because I was hemorrhaging under my skin, and the blood was trying to find a place to go. ITP is a blood disease that causes your blood to become thin like water, and it fails to coagulate or clot, which is needful if one becomes injured.

You may be saying, that I should have known that something was wrong, and maybe you're right. But as a man, because I was not in pain, I thought I was okay, and most men are just like me, we want to wait to the last minute to go to the doctor, when we could go while the sickness is still minor. Because of my stubbornness, even though I had unexplained bruises on my upper and lower body, I found myself coughing up blood in February of 2013.

I thank God for a praying wife. Having a praying wife is probably what helped saved my life. Because I didn't know that I was that sick, (due to the Glory) my spirit had overtaken everything that was going on in my body. Because I didn't know I was sick, I kept running full speed , between ministry and my job. I would work 10-12 hours a day at Fed Ex, and come to the church for a few hours each day. We had planned a family week at the Church for the week of February 18-22, which meant every night that week, there would be ministry going on, for couples, singles, men, women, and children. Five straight nights of ministry, after working five ten- hour days is what I had dialed up. This was a good thing, this was a Godly thing, this was a positive thing; and after all, this was ministry.

What could possibly go wrong with doing ministry, and advancing the Kingdom? One problem, I was two months into a teaching series on "the Glory of God". My Spirit forgot to inform my body to that it was getting ready to accelerate, it was like pressing the gas and burning rubber on a set of bald tires.....it was just a matter of time.

In other words, as sick as I was, I should have been feeling fatigue, or weak, or tired, instead it was just the opposite. Because of the teaching on "The Glory", my body was starting to be energize by the (Glory) atmosphere of heaven. Instead of slowing down, I was actually speeding up, and guess what, I was playing right into the devil's hand. I later realized that the devil was trying to kill me, by using something that he knew I was passionate about...ministry. You see, the "Glory Of God" will cause you to have an out of body experience. That is exactly what was going on with me, and that's one of the "hidden dangers" of the Glory.

The human body is made up of cells, for the most part. We have red blood cells, (they help carry oxygen in the blood); we have white blood cells, (they help fight off infections); and we have blood platelets, (platelets cause coagulation, or clotting which the blood must have). When someone is cut or injured, what causes the bleeding to slow down or eventually stop, are the platelets doing their job. The platelets rush to the injured place and start to clot that place up. My platelets were being removed from my body, now we had to figured out why.

GLORY CAN CAUSE YOU TO HAVE AN OUT OF BODY EXPERIENCE

NATURAL REVELATION

First of all, I certainly want to be clear, that I applaud education. I am an extremist when it comes to gaining a higher level of education. Starting wherever you may be in life, pick yourself up, and go back to school. Go get that trade, that GED, that Associates, Bachelors, Masters, or Doctorate degree.... Again I applaud education. But here's my big point, there is a knowledge above college.

I know many well-educated people, who are so educated, to the point where they rationalize everything. I have even had people to tell me that if it does not add up on paper, or if it does not seem logical, they simply cannot believe God for it. So don't allow all of your human knowledge to keep from believing God to heal, save, deliver, and set free. The scriptures teach us that the carnal mind is enmity against God, (Romans 8:7). If all you have is earthly knowledge, chances are you will not experience the level of GLORY that I'm speaking, until.......God allows you to have an encounter with him, (I almost started preaching right there).

SPIRITUAL REVELATION

The apostle Paul made this statement in 2 Corinthians 12: 2, " I knew a man in Christ above fourteen, (whether in the body, I cannot tell; or whether out of the body, I cannot tell: God knoweth;) such an one got caught up in the third heavens.

The Message Bible: Paul says "You've forced me to talk this way, and I do it against my better judgment. But now that we're at it, I may as well bring up the matter of visions and revelations that God gave me. For instance, I know a man who, fourteen years ago, was seized by Christ, and swept in Ecstasy to the heights of heaven. I really don't know if this took place in the body or out of it; only God knows. I know that this man was hijacked into Paradise- again, whether in or out of the body, I don't know, God knows.

I did not know it at the time, but because our beloved church family, New Destiny, was being saturated with a very heavy dose of teaching on the subject, "A Greater Passion For A Greater Glory", I say this with all humility, the people were getting the message, and they were grasping the word. After five months of non-stop teaching on the GLORY, the enemy's worst nightmare happened. The Church was now hungry for the GLORY of GOD. They wanted to experience the GLORY, after hearing about the atmosphere of heaven, how Jesus brought the environment of heaven to every place he trod, and how He was the Brightness of the Glory of God. They understood that the Glory that I spoke of is available to every born again believer, and they were willing to make the adjustments in their lives, and to do whatever it took to experience that Glory!

New Destiny quickly recognize that God has tipped us off and had given us a revelation of what's was about to happen, when He super-naturally kept me alive, when the doctors said I was so close to death. It was that revelation on the GLORY, that I am still preaching about five months later. The GLORY allowed my Spirit, to overtake all my natural body, and never even allow my body to feel sick. This is the GLORY that I want the world to know about!

MOSES ASKED GOD "SHOW ME YOUR GLORY'

In Exodus 33, Moses asked God to "Show me your Glory". He had already seen the hand of God. He saw Him part the Red Sea, turn water into blood, bring water out of the rock, rain down manna from heaven and perform miracles in Egypt, but still he asked God to "Show him His Glory". I said all this to say that THERE IS MORE!

When I became sick, I had become so consumed with the Glory of God, until I was experiencing an out of body experience and I was not even aware of it. I was literally so close to death, that my body should have shut itself down already, but instead, we had now tapped into the GLORY, "the environment of heaven". Looking back at the situation, I realize now, it could have gone another way, but I'm still here only by the Grace of God!

Once you tap into the Glory of God, everything does not have to change, but the way you see things about your life begins to change. The weightiness of God, now begins to rest on your life as well as the ministry. I wrote this book to bring about more awareness of the GLORY OF GOD. Miracles still takes place today; God is still the same God now as He was in biblical days. God wants to move in the earth realm today as he moved in the Bible, but there must be a people who believe in the supernatural power of God.

I am ALIVE today because of the GLORY of GOD. I will forever tell of his greatness and His wonder working Power. I recognize that I was hand selected to go through a "season of sickness" not because God was mad at me, but rather God knew I would give Him the GLORY! The GLORY that I'm speaking of is not only resting on me personally but I have decreed and declared the this same GLORY also is resting on our congregation.

I asked God to "Show me His Glory", and now I understand why Moses added in Exodus 33:13, "If I've found grace in your sight, show me your way". It still causes me to tremble when I think about that statement. You see if I had not found grace in God's eyes, I could not have withstood the weight of his GLORY, it was not the doctors or the medicine, but rather it was the GLORY that kept me alive. The spirit of Glory is resting on our ministry. I recognize it, as do others, that the GLORY of God is in our midst.

For example, financially we as a church are experiencing the supernatural corporately as the ministry has now broken ground on a brand new facility that is due to be completed very soon; all to the GLORY belongs to God. Once you begin to embrace the GLORY everything about your life and ministry begins to change. Once you step into the Glory, you quickly recognize that the demonic forces you are facing now are far more intense than what you faced in the past. You must, and I repeat this, you must be spiritually alert and tuned in to where God is and what He's saying to you. Even though you know God spoke to you, you heard him clearly, it is not ever easy, if it's really a God-sized assignment. The greater the revelation, the more the enemy will torment you. There are many voices that will come to you to try to discourage you from your assignment. Stand your ground and trust that if God called you to it, He will bring you through it! Again, I'm alive because of the GLORY of GOD!

THE GLORY WILL BE CONTAGIOUS

For example, there was a baby pronounced dead at one of our local hospitals. One of our members was related to the baby. When she called my wife and I to tell us the bad news, she was on her way to the hospital. She asked what she should do once she arrived at the hospital to be with her family. My wife told her to go in the emergency room and pray over the baby.

When she arrived at the hospital, she met the baby's father who was distraught as anyone would be, on the floor, sobbing at the news of his little baby. She walked past the father into the room where the lifeless baby was lying. As she began to pray over the baby as my wife Rita had instructed her to do. The baby began to move. Today, that little baby is fine, and living a normal life, because of the GLORY.

There's another lady in our church , who moved to Alabama because of a job transition. When she moved to Gadsden she was single, backslidden, and still in search of something from the Lord. She was in search of the Glory. We all know what it's like to be in a new city, with no family in that city, and you are trying to find a place to worship. She visited church after church looking for the place of worship that was the right fit for her and her family.

I watched her come in on Sundays and Wednesday hungry, thirsty, and in search of something more. I still remember the day she got up out of her seat, and walked down the aisle as we made the alter call, and extended the invitation to become a member of New Destiny.

When she joined our church she was already saved, and her father was also a minister of fifty years. But why did she move to Alabama is the question. In reality, it was not simply to relocate, God had an assignment on her life. But her obedience was the key factor in God bringing about the manifestation in her life.

To make a long story short, because she obeyed God, and submitted to the vision of the house, without fully understanding it all, she is now positioned to be a blessing to the body of Christ. She went through new member's class; she went through our minister's training course, and became actively involved in ministry. She is now a part of our intercessory prayer team. She is restored back to the pulpit. She is happily married. She retired early from her job which included benefits. Her children have also followed her and relocated to Alabama, and they are also become members of our church. She and her husband have closed on their new home, all because of the GLORY!

Whatever God is speaking to you about, it's time to stop wrestling with it, stop trying to figure out how God is going to do it, just trust God and obey. As my Pastor, Dr. R.A. Vernon would say, "just bust a move".

3

THE GLORY COMES WITH A PRICE

"I refuse to give God that which cost me nothing". I want to make it crystal clear that to walk in the level of Glory that I'm speaking of is going to come with a price. What are you willing to give up to follow Jesus. What changes are you willing to make to become a recipient of this Glory that I'm speaking of. I spent a year in sickness, waiting and believing God for the manifestation of my healing. I would have loved for it to happen in a day, a week, or even a month, but that was not the case. God was doing a work in my life that I would never be able to forget. I did not realize what all came along with my request for the Glory. I thought it was just another year with a new theme, but God had other plans.

Every year, I would begin the New Year by teaching a new series which usually is our Church's theme for the remainder of the year. In 2013, I began a brand new series called, "A Greater Passion For A Greater Glory". Little did I know that my request for more of the Glory, would come with a very expensive price tag.

Let me be tell you, not from what I've read or heard, but what I've experienced, the Glory will cost you something. You have probably looked at people that God is clearly using and thought about how you want to be used. You look at the external Glory and think how much you want God to use you. What you don't see, though, is the cost. If I could give only one piece of advice to anyone in ministry, especially pastors, I would tell them that godliness with contentment is a great gain. The Apostle Paul stated in Philippians 4:11, "I have learned to be content, in whatever state that I am in." You will not come to experience God on a deeper level, with Him unfolding mysteries and sharing revelations; you will not see the arm of the Lord revealed to you or experience the supernatural power of God, you will not know him in a more intimate way, without God allowing you to go through trials that will literally test your faith and see if you really trust God the way you claim.

It is easy to praise the Lord when everything is going well, too. It's easy to be grateful when all of your bills are paid, there are no doctor's visits and health issues looming. But what if all that changed without any warning?

Have you ever looked at a situation in your life and wondered how you ended up where you did? One of those times when you did everything you were supposed to do. You know you're not perfect but you lived for God, avoided bringing reproach to the name of the Lord, tried to serve Him wholeheartedly. Still, with all this, you found yourself or a family member suffering in some way, experiencing some kind of affliction. If your answer is yes, then that means you may be a candidate to experience the Glory of God.

YOU ARE A CANDIDATE TO BRING GOD GLORY?

Job was a prime candidate when God was looking for someone that He could "set up" to see His Glory. As the Bible says in Job, chapter 42, verse 10, "God blessed Job with twice as much as he had in the beginning".

Now we know we don't serve God for what He can do for us. We serve Him because we love Him, and because of who He is. But I must say, it is wonderful to know we serve the living God and He loves his children so much that He will sometimes hand select them to go through certain trials, for one purpose, He wants to get Glory from that situation when it's all said and done. That is what He got from Job and that is what He wants from you and me.

I can't speak for anyone else. I can only speak for myself, but I am determined to bless the Lord when I'm up, and when I'm down. I am determined to bless Him when I can see Him, and even when I cannot trace Him at all.

I want to encourage someone who may be on the verge of quitting or someone who may be doubting God. I want to encourage you to shake yourself loose, get a praise on your lips; shout unto God, and let the devil hear you sending SOUNDWAVES. THERE WILL BE GLORY AFTER THIS! MANY WILL BE CONVERTED BY YOUR TESTIMONY.

I have always had a clean bill of health. I have always been athletic. I grew up playing football, from pee-wee league to college. I ran track, even. As an adult, I am a non-smoker and a non-drinker. I eat pretty well and drink water every morning. I get plenty of fresh air, too, after I wake up in the mornings.

However, as I began this teaching series, "A Greater Passion For A Greater Glory," we began to experience a tremendous outpouring of the presence of God in a way we never had since the inception of our ministry. I mean you could walk into the sanctuary and just feel the Shekinah Glory (that tangible presence of God). You knew when the praise and worship began, that it was going to be one of those days, where there's no telling what will take place in the service, but it will be awesome. And I began to ask God to show us His Glory. We were praying for more of God.

Since January 1st, we set out to show God just how hungry we were for him. As stated earlier, we were not looking for stuff, or material things. We wanted Him. We opened up the doors of New Destiny for prayer Monday – Saturday and assigned prayer warriors every hour to be on post. You see I know that to advance the Kingdom of God, loose the bands of wickedness, open the eyes of the blind, see the lame walk, and to experience the supernatural power of God, it was going to cost us something. I have always had this saying, and it's worth repeating, "I will not give God that which cost me nothing".

THE "GLORY" CAUSES DEMONS TO TREMBLE

When you begin to hunger and thirst more of His Glory, I would encourage you to have a team of intercessors around you, those who have the call of intercession on their life. There are some areas in the church where you can have people just fill in where there are vacancies. Trust me, this is not one of them. Because when you ask God to reveal His Glory to you, the enemy becomes afraid of you, not because of you, but because you represent, the Lord God Almighty. The enemy knows you are a threat to the kingdom of darkness, once you become knowledgeable of the GLORY. He knows you can and will disrupt demonic activity, eliminate satanic influence, and at the same time advance the Kingdom of God, Hallelujah!

If you are serious about the GLORY, you MUST have a team of intercessors around you, covering you around the clock as he (the enemy) will throw everything he can against you, your family, your spouse, your children, your health, and all that you have to make you back away from the GLORY. You must be determined as Paul was in Romans 8:31, "that if God be for me, who can be against me". Let's get ready for this journey, as the Holy Spirit leads me to share my personal experience from what I've learned from living in the atmosphere of the GLORY OF GOD, and most of all, what I can now tell you that God will do for us, when we thrust ourselves into the atmosphere of heaven A.K.A., the "Glory Of God".

Left: Chief Thoracic Surgeon Dan Miller removed mass from heart and lungs
Right: Tennis ball size mass (Thymoma); (Emory Hospital, Atlanta)

 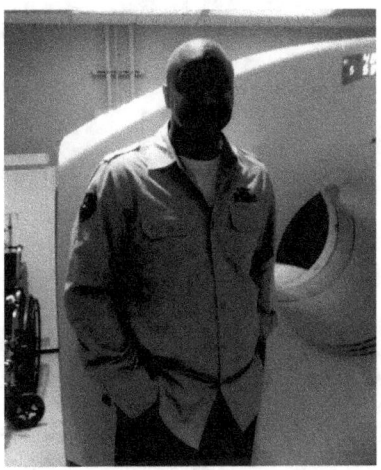

Left: MRSA Staph Infection Gadsden Regional Hospital
Right: PET Scan Before Heart Surgery; (Emory Hospital, Atlanta)

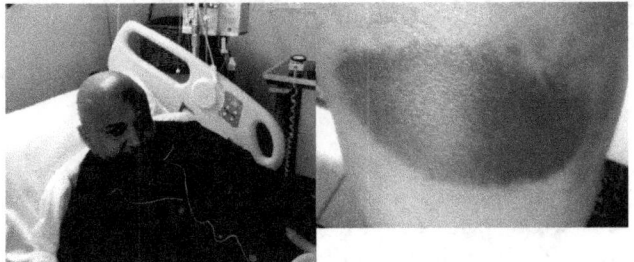

Left: Blood Platelet Transfusion Gadsden Regional Hospital
Right: (ITP) Thrombocytopenia Bruises all over my body

4

"NOT UNTO DEATH"

When Jesus finally did get to Bethany, the hometown of Mary, Martha, and Lazarus, his friend was pronounced dead already. As a matter a fact Jesus shows up four days after he died, by design. He waited until everybody was made aware of Lazarus death. But initially, (while Lazarus was still barely alive) when He heard of Lazarus's sickness, this was his response: "This sickness is not unto death, but for the Glory of God, that the son of God may be Glorified through it", King James Version, John 11:4)

Let me explain why I wrote this chapter and shared the graphic details about my sickness. First and foremost, God was using my sickness to get Glory through it. Secondly, through my own infirmities and sickness, God has revealed to me that the church needs a checkup, some treatments, and maybe some surgeries to correct some of its problems. The problems within the body are not just going to disappear whether it be the natural or the spiritual.

During my sickness and all my diagnoses, I discovered a strange parallel within the spiritual and natural body. The first order of business was to find out what was wrong with me (my body). We now know I have a blood disease called ITP, which is an autoimmune disease. The next thing we had to find was the cause of the ITP. We now know there is no known cause of the disease.

Next we had to figure out the why. In other words, why did this happen. Ultimately, God was using this sickness to bring Himself GLORY. There were parts of my body that were attacking other parts of my body. So I'm reminded of what Paul said, "first the natural, then the spiritual. Howbeit that was not first which is spiritual, but that which is natural; and afterward that which is spiritual", (1 Corinthians 15:46)

In a previous chapter, I shared with you about how we came to discover my sickness, and ultimately what was wrong with me. Keep in mind, the whole while that this sickness was invading my body, I was already several months into this teaching on the GLORY. We learned on Sunday, February 17, that I had a very rare blood disease called Immune Thrombocytopenic Purpura (ITP). How rare was it you may be asking. ITP is so rare that the hospital where I was being treated had never treated a patient with my condition. That's when you know you need the Holy Ghost, because we need revelation from on high. I had questions, but there were only few answers from the doctors I was seeing.

What I love about God, though, is that He never leaves his children in the dark. Listen at what the Lord told Ananias about Saul before He used Saul and changed his name from Saul to Paul." But the Lord said unto him, Go thy way: for he is a chosen vessel unto me, to bear my name before the Gentiles, and kings, and the children of Israel: For I will shew him how great things HE MUST SUFFER for my name's sake" (Acts 9:15).

My big point here is, God tipped Saul off that He was going to use him mightily, but Saul was going to have to suffer for Christ sake. I'm telling you this for a reason, because if you know why you're going through a situation, your circumstances may not change immediately, but it makes it a little easier to endure.

DON'T DISCOUNT YOUR DREAMS

I make this statement from time to time to the members of New Destiny, "documentation beats conversation". What is so ironic about the doctor visit on February 17, is that I discovered that I was suffering from, or should have been suffering from Thrombocytopenia. But (because I was in the Glory realm) the effects of the disease were not there. I mean I had the physical markings all over my body, but at a time when I should have been weak, tired, and feeling faint, the "Glory" had me energized, and my adrenalin was flowing. Remember I had already been to three services, and was preparing for our first ever "Family Week." This is how you know the devil is ruthless and don't play fair. Consider this: three services on Sunday, then I scheduled five straight nights of ministry, which I was planning to attend, I would have been dead before Friday.... but I was in the "GLORY", Hallelujah! And so Monday morning after my visit with my personal doctor, I was admitted into the hospital for five days, and given a blood platelet transfusion.

But that Sunday night, before I was admitted in the hospital, God already revealed this sickness to my wife in a dream, (which happened to be on January 17) that didn't make any sense at the time. That's why it's good to have an intercessory prayer team around you. They are able to come together in prayer, and seek God on the matter. And the Lord will give the interpretation of the dream. Even though the dream didn't make any sense, my wife wrote it all down and sent it to our prayer warriors to pray over along with her, for more revelation. That's why I say documentation beats conversation, because God would eventually tie this all together where it would make sense, but it would be months later.

LADY RITA'S DREAM

This is how it all unfolded. On January 17, my wife had a dream. In the dream, my wife saw me walking up our driveway, when out of nowhere, a wolf jumped out of the woods and began to attack me. As I was being attacked by this wolf, there was a lot of panic and commotion. She said the next thing she saw was a police car, driving extremely fast trying to make up to our driveway to bring order to the chaos. But before the authorities could reach my driveway, my wife sees this huge lion, which came from nowhere and began to attack the wolf. She then notices in the dream that there was blood, and it was coming from one of my hands. As she yells to get my attention, she says there is blood dripping from your hand. But she says I began to look at the wound, and then tell my wife, don't worry about it, "I can shake it off," then I began to shake my hand up and down and all the bleeding began to stop. She says that's the last thing she remembers before waking up. And from February to now, we've been shaking it off. This was God's way of giving us REVELATION of my bleeding condition, which we now know as ITP.

Twelve months later, I can look back at the dream with more clarity, and see what God was saying back in January. The full revelation and interpretation of the dream he showed my wife was this, "Therefore his sisters sent unto him, saying, Lord, behold, he whom thou lovest is sick. When Jesus heard that, he said, This sickness is not unto death, but for the glory of God, that the Son of God might be glorified thereby", (John 11:3-4).

BLOOD PLATELET TRANSFUSION

My platelet count was eleven when I was admitted into the hospital in February, and had to be given a blood platelet transfusion to get platelets back inside my body as quickly as possible. Keep in mind that platelet transfusions are only given in emergency situations where there is bleeding from an open wound or the body has depleted them somehow. That may not mean much to you if you're not familiar with platelets, white blood cells, and red blood cells. A normal, healthy person has a platelet count with a range of 150-400 thousand platelets. That initial doctor visit revealed I only had 11 thousand platelets (almost none). So for me to be walking around with a platelet count of 11 thousand meant I was a walking time bomb, with the threat of bleeding from the brain. That's why I had to be quickly admitted into the hospital and given a transfusion.

Remember, though, I was also consumed with the "GLORY", and the GLORY (environment of heaven) did not inform my body that it was under attack, it simply went into protective mode. And after five days in the hospital, just like in the dream, because of the GLORY, I was able to "shake it off."

IMMUNOGLOBULIN INJECTION (IVIG)

I have come to realize since this sickness invaded my body, that there are a lot of sick people in this world, fighting for their health and their life. I decided to openly talk about what I've been through to hopefully create more sensitivity for those individuals who are not well. And also maybe to educate others of some of the medicine and means of treatments that I have personally experienced this year alone (2013).

IVIG was one of the first means of treatment we tried to get my ITP under control. IVIG is a blood product extracted from plasma from blood donors, then administered intravenously. I spent the first four months in the Cancer center receiving IMMUNOGLOBULIN treatments intravenously. Each treatment for me would take about five to seven hours at a time.

After I would receive these treatments, they would boost my platelet count up to a safe range. The problem with IVIG Treatments was, it would take seven hours to receive a single treatment, but it would only last in my body for a month. After a month, my platelets would drop again. I had to continue this cycle of treatments, but I was not getting better.

DECADRON INJECTIONS

DECADRON is a corticosteroid, which is similar to a natural hormone. Decadron was the first of several steroids we tried to help elevate my platelets. It proved to be effective as far as getting my platelets up, but I could not handle the many side effects of Decadron. The inability to sleep, the chemo hiccups, inability to remember things, the nausea, and the worst of all the side effects, was the hallucinating it caused. I requested to be taken off Decadron.

PREDNISONE TREATMENTS

PREDNISONE is another medication which has been used to treat leukemia and to relieve rheumatic and allergic conditions. Prednisone is also used to treat the symptoms of certain types of cancers. Prednisone has been referred to by many as a miracle drug. In my own personal situation, I have what is called an autoimmune disease. When you have an autoimmune disease, it means your immune system is so aggressive that it attacks other areas in the body. In my case, my immune system do not recognize my platelets. They are perceived as being foreign, therefore they are constantly being destroyed by my immune system.

Prednisone is a potent corticosteroid that I have to take to protect my platelets. Prednisone weakened my immune system to keep my immune system from attacking my platelets. The problem with that was once the Prednisone did it job, my platelets count would go up, but my immune system, which was weakened by design by the Prednisone, could no longer fight off infections and diseases. I know right, but I was still in the "Glory." Large dosages of Prednisone is what opened the door to me getting a staph infection. Prednisone weakens the immune system.

BONE MARROW BIOPSY

You may be wondering why I'm having to have a bone marrow biopsy done. Usually if someone is having a bone marrow done, the doctor has reason to believe there is cancer or leukemia. This is done for several reasons, but let me explain my situation, which by the way is totally spiritual. The purpose of me having a bone marrow biopsy was to determine if my body is producing platelets. Platelets are produced inside the bone marrow. The biopsy revealed that my body was in fact producing platelets. Once we knew that my body was producing platelets, the next step was to determine what was destroying my platelets. So first, we had a test done to check my spleen. The spleen has been known to hold platelets hostage inside the body. The doctors determined that the spleen appeared to be functioning normally. So all and all, it was good to have that bone marrow biopsy done, because it told us what we needed to know.

Let me be the first to say, out of the eight times I had been admitted into the hospital in 2013, the bone marrow biopsy still remained the most painful, horrifying visit of them all. Whenever there is a problem with the blood, you'll eventually end up in the hands of an oncologist or hematologist. And so after CT scans, CAT scan, and x-rays, the bone marrow is also necessary. If you have a bone marrow biopsy, there is a reason for it. In my case, we were looking for platelet production. There are other reasons for bone marrow exams, as I stated earlier, such as looking for leukemia or cancer. I would eventually have many more procedures done, but the bone marrow is performed by cutting a hole into the skin, drilling a hole into your bone, in my case, into my pelvic, and inserting a huge needle into the bone to snatch away parts of the bone marrow. Did I mention that this is all done while you are awake? Exactly, even after the deadening, it was still excruciating pain I'm so glad I was in the GLORY, Hallelujah!

MASS FOUND ON HEART

I believe I've already explained to you what it means to be stoned. It carries with it the connotation of dealing with multiple problems at the same time. As if it were not already bad enough having finally agreed to go forward with the bone marrow biopsy, the very same day of the bone marrow procedure, while I was still being cleaned up from that procedure, another doctor walks in and hands my wife a piece of paper. He Then stated, "oh by the way, our x-rays show us there is a mass in front of his heart. We feel that it needs to be removed immediately.

At this time, I'm starting to feel like Job, who had to receive one bad report after another. I'll bet Job was thinking to himself, don't nobody else bring me no more bad news. The devil even knows the truth of the matter. That even he cannot get to us, nor lay a hand on us, unless God remove, or put a breach in the hedge.

"Hast not thou made an hedge about him, and about his house, and about all that he hath on every side? thou hast blessed the work of his hands, and his substance is increased in the land", (Job 1:10). It's was encouraging for me, even when I found out about the mass, that it could not be so, unless God allowed it, and besides I'm still "In The Glory. Therefore I had a word, " I could shake it off!"

HEART SURGERY

After giving it a lot of thought and meditating on it in prayer, I decided on a thoracic surgeon. The local doctors felt like the mass in front of my heart may be related to the ITP. We traveled to Birmingham and the doctor in Birmingham told me to use the best doctors available. They referred me to Emory or Vanderbilt as the two places to go if I elected not to use them (UAB).

My wife and I chose Dr. Daniel Miller at Emory in Atlanta to have my heart surgery. After meeting with the surgeon and his staff, I decided to go through with it. Thank God, I was "In The Glory". My heart surgery was scheduled for May 14, 2013.

So we decided to go to Atlanta early, get settled in, and get mentally prepared for this operation. By now you know, the devil don't play fair. The enemy tried to kill me in the middle of the night. He didn't want me to go through with this procedure, because we later found out it was 7 cm, (the size of a tennis ball) still growing and cancerous. Somebody should be shouting with me, Hallelujah!

So the devil tried to kill me in the middle of the night, as I began to experience serious migraine headaches, which is not good for someone like me, with a bleeding disorder. To make a long story short, my wife panicked, called back to Alabama and my Hematologist told her to get me to the hospital ASAP. It was about 3:00 o'clock in the morning.

My wife has stood right by my side. As I lay there in the hospital at Emory, looking at my poor wife who had to fall asleep sitting up in a chair in a dark room in the middle of the night, alone, miles away from home, I cried. Here we are in Atlanta, coming over early to get rested up and prepared for my heart surgery, and end up in the hospital. But I had a word to stand on now: "I could shake it off."

On Tuesday, a few days later, I had heart surgery. It went very well. The mass was removed. There were no major complications, except the surgeon had to make an additional incision, due to the Thymoma (mass) being larger than we thought. Other than that the surgery itself went well, because the Lord was operating on me, Glory to God. We later found out, I still had platelet problems but I had a word to stand on, I could "shake it off!"

CANCER

I've learned to count my blessings. Sometimes you may not understand how a person who is already sick, can find a reason to still give God Praise. Well consider this, it may very well be that the person realizes that, it may be bad, but it could be worse. That's the way I feel, I simply cannot complain when I see how The GLORY shielded me from the agonizing torment. There is a torment that only a cancer patient can understand because it's in their body. Another reason I praise God the way I do is He kept my mind off the thought of it being cancerous, because I did not know it, until they removed it.

Just when you think things could not possibly get any worse, the devil is still throwing everything he possibly can at me. After the surgery was over, and the tennis ball size Thymoma (mass) was removed, it had to be sent to the lab as we waited on the pathology report. Only then was it revealed to me that the Thymoma was cancerous. Here's the shouting part, the cancerous Thymoma which was removed from between my heart and lungs was completely encapsulated. In other words it was as if the GLORY of GOD had it concealed inside of a Ziploc bag, not allowing it to infiltrate into my heart and lungs. Let me stop for a minute so I can take "PRAISE BREAK."

CHEMOTHERAPY

After being hospitalized two more times, due to low platelets, it was time to find a new hematologist. We found a doctor we were comfortable with at UAB Kirkland Clinic, Dr. Uma Borate. We decided to try another method of treatment in the form of a chemo drug. It was not just any drug, though. It was the very dangerous, and potent drug, called Rituxan.

Rituxan has been known to eliminate platelet problems for life but the drawback is the side effects. Rituxan is such a dangerous drug, I had to sign a consent form because people have died during treatment. Imagine this, you are getting prepared for treatment and the health educator gives you your pamphlet explaining the risk. And in the very first paragraph, it reads as follows: Most people who died from Rituxan died within 24 hours, or during the first treatment."

By the grace of God, we made it through four treatments of Rituxan. Only to discover later, that my platelets would drop again two months later.

STAPH INFECTION

At this point in my life, I am totally convinced that this is a spiritual encounter, being played out in the natural realm, and my body has been selected as the battleground. As I'm writing this chapter of the book, I am at home still in isolation. Why is that? Because I was admitted back into the hospital for the eighth time in 2013, this time for five days. I was also hospitalized two months ago at UAB, and treated for what I thought was a spider bite. Well, I now have come to know that my last two hospital visits were due to a very dangerous, contagious, and painful staph infection known as MRSA.

MRSA can affect the skin, surgical wounds, urinary tracts, lungs and nasal passageway, and other areas. Methicillin Resistant Staphylococcus Aureus (MRSA) infection is so dangerous because it does respond to most antibiotics. So after five days in Gadsden Regional, and now two more weeks of antibiotics at home, it still feels like I'm in isolation.

Still, I cannot have any contact with people, and still having to sterilize everything, after having our entire house completely sanitize. This year of sickness in 2013 has been one I will never forget. And as I stated earlier, I recognize that it is all spiritual.

God allowed the hedge to be breached for a reason. It is now December, God tipped us off in January. I have seen it all this year, and I am alive to talk about it.

I feel blessed that I was chosen to go through this. God knew that I would tell the world about his saving power. He knew I would encourage others while I was going through chemo, that He Lives. God placed me right there among people who were terminally ill to speak a word of hope to them. "But he was wounded for our transgressions, he was bruised for our iniquities: the chastisement of our peace was upon him; and with his stripes we are healed" (Isaiah 53:5).

CONCLUSION: Just as I have shared with you how some of the problems that I have experienced, was simply because my own body was launching an all-out attack against itself. Let's take heed, fix the problem by getting to the root of the situation that we may continue to advance the Kingdom, in Jesus Name.

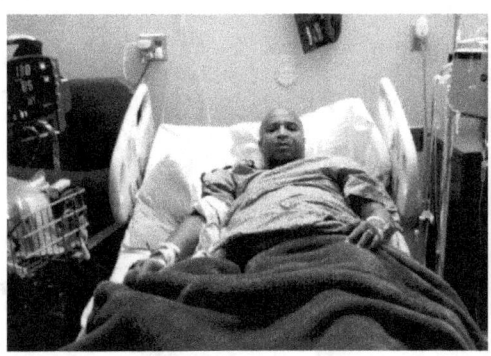

Gadsden Regional Hospital Immunoglobin Treatments

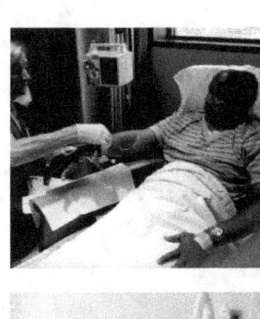
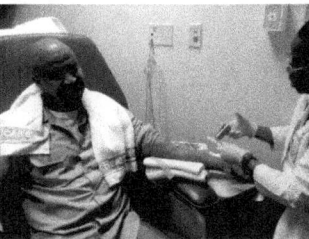
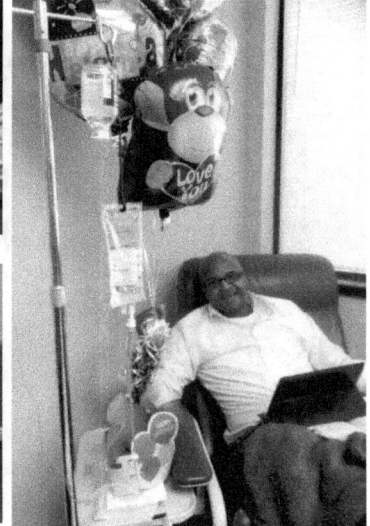
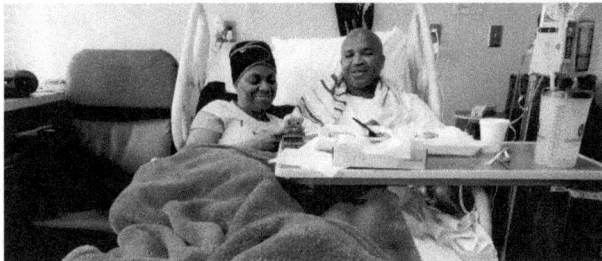

My Birthday at the Cancer Center IVIG Treatments

5

THERE ARE BENEFITS OF BEING IN THE GLORY

All of us who choose to live Godly will suffer persecution, and as I stated before, I myself am in the middle of a storm. The winds are blowing, the sea is raging, and at times the cloud seem to be dark, "but I know that my redeemer liveth, and He shall stand at the latter day upon the earth", (Job 19:25). I am a living witness today that are benefits to making your abode in the "GLORY."

You have to remind yourself, that no matter what it looks like, no matter what the doctor's report is, no matter how you may be feeling, this too shall pass, and there will be Glory after this. Too often, we read the first chapter of Job, and we see all the things Job went through. We see how he lost his children, his cattle, his possessions, and even his health. And before we point fingers at Mrs. Job, stop for a minute, let me give you something to meditate on. These were not only Job's children, cattle, and possessions, but these were her children also. So we are always so hard on his wife, as if what she said didn't make sense, but she had to watch her children die and then also watch her husband suffer. Another thing we need to remember is that when you and I are in a trial or just having a bad day, it easy for us to pick up the Bible and just turn to a passage of the scripture. We can find comfort in reading the Word of God. Well, Job did not have the same privilege as we do today, because He did not have the written Bible as we do, yet he still held on to his integrity.

Job said, "naked I came out of my Mother's womb, and naked shall I return. Blessed be the name of the Lord", (Job 1:21). Job was not concerned about material things, or his substance, or the abundance of all his wealth. He trusted God in the midst of it all.

So if you're reading this book, and you in a trial, don't just read the first few chapters of the book of Job and stop there. You see after God saw the integrity of Job's heart and how Job held on to his integrity, God monitored his every move. Sometimes we fail to recognize that God sees us when no one else does, and He knows whether or not He can trust us with the Glory. You see it's been thousands of years now, but people are still talking about Job. Why? Because his story really shows us the heart of God. Let's look at a few things here.

JOB'S STORY IS ALL ABOUT GLORY

1. We see that the enemy, walks to and fro in the earth, seeking whom he may devour, (Job 1:7).
2. We see that God decides, who he can mess with, and God sometimes allow it, (Job 1:8).
3. We see that God also sets the boundaries, what he can and cannot do, (Job 1:12).
4. We see that when the enemy has bothered you enough, God stops him, (Job 42:7).
5. We see that God is looking for someone who will bring Him Glory, (Job 1).
6. We see that you cannot serve this awesome God, and He not prolong your days, (Job 42:16).
7. We also see in chapter 42, that God will give you double for all your trouble.

THE GLORY ALLOWS YOU TO SEE ON THE OTHER SIDE

Even as I write this book, today is my birthday; it's March 20, 2013. It is 3:00 p.m. and I'm at the cancer center. I have been here since 9:00 a.m. receiving IVIG, and Decadron (steroids). I still have another two hours before I'm done. Trust me when I tell you that my passion has brought me some pain, but God. You can be a born again believer, and attend church, and just be a satisfied Christian. But I always want more of God, more word, more of his presence, and certainly more of his Glory. I just want more of Him. And even though I've had to spend my birthday at the hospital, not just at the hospital, but at the cancer center, because the blood doctors and cancer doctors (Hematologist & Oncologist) both work from the same unit.

THE GLORY WILL KEEP YOUR MIND!

Talk about pain, only God knows the thoughts you have to battle with in your mind. Every time I go to the restroom, the signs on the door says "chemo patients only". When I drive through the parking lots of this building, the parking spaces have signs that read, "cancer patients only". Needless to say, I have to constantly remind the devil that he is a liar, and the father of lies, and there is no truth him, nor is he is capable of telling the truth. I walk in these restroom and remind the devil that I am completely healed in JESUS'S Name!

On the week of my birthday, this was the time I had to rely on the "atmosphere of heaven" (the GLORY) more so than any other time. You may be wondering why at a time like this, because this is normally a time of celebration, friends and family, gifts and cards, and to hear from all well-wishers, and by all means, please understand that I received my share of all that. I truly have the most amazing family, and that includes my church family. New Destiny has been a God send for my wife and me during this trial, and I am eternally grateful, but this is why the word of God tells us to gird up the loins of our minds.

I was originally scheduled for 8 weeks of blood work, which happened to be at the Cancer Center after the first month of treatments. Things appeared to be going according to plan, but always remember that the devil won't play fair.

Since my platelets dropped to 11,000 in February, I had received transfusions, steroid injections, IVIG treatments, weekly visits to the doctor to have my blood platelets checked. All through the month of February they were going up each week. They went up from 11K, to 60K, to 120K, to 356k. Then to get into March, and just when it seems like things were looking up, I went to the doctor on March 19th, (the day before my birthday) which was my routine visit, only to find that my platelets were bottomed out again. This meant that the rest of the week would have to be spent at the hospital, receiving treatments all over again, as I did in February. It also meant five hospital visits on the week of my birthday, eight hours of treatment on my birthday, a trip to Atlanta to Emory Hospital, then back to Gadsden Regional that Friday.

These treatments happened because I had already consulted with three different hospitals, Gadsden Regional, UAB Birmingham, and Emory Hospital, Atlanta, to see about heart surgery to remove a mass from my heart, that, incidentally, was found when my platelets dropped, and a series of tests were run - talk about "A Price For The Glory."

THE GLORY WILL PROTECT YOU

Again I want to say, I had to stay focused on the word God gave me at the first of the year, " A Greater Passion, For A Greater Glory". There are some things that are just not important when your life or health are at stake. My prayer and desperate plea was still the same, "Lord, show me your GLORY!"

You must have enough of the WORD in you that is able to sustain you in times like these, and also to remind yourself, why you are going through whatever situation you are going through. There is always a reason for it. Is God trying to tell you something? Is He trying to show you something? Or is He just using you as a faith partner in the earth, to bring Him GLORY? Whatever the case, don't fall into the traps and lies of the devil, and remember the "the thief cometh but not to steal, kill, and destroy, but I am come that you might have LIFE, and life more abundantly," (John 10:10).

Remember to pray, read your word, and fast. I can't emphasize this enough, surround yourself with a team of intercessors, who are spiritual-minded, who have a relationship with God and knows how to get in touch with Him.

6

"I WAS IN THE RIGHT PLACE AT THE RIGHT TIME"

I want to thank my Lord and Savior Jesus Christ, for giving me an ear to hear. I heard God clearly when He told me at our Watch Night service to get in the GLORY. I was in "The right place at the right time". It's comforting to know that we serve a God who knows everything concerning us. The fact that he made us, and he knows, tells me He knows how much we are able to bear. Furthermore, once we have reached our limit and allowed God to finish his purpose in us, He will bring us out.

" But the God of all grace, who hath called us unto his eternal glory by Christ Jesus, after that ye have suffered a while, make you perfect, establish, strengthen, settle you. To him be glory and dominion forever and ever". Amen. (King James Version, 1 Peter 5:10-11).

I have also grown to know that one word from the Lord can change your entire life. That's why the Word of God let's us know how important it is to hear or read the right word for your current situation.

"A man hath joy by the answer of his mouth: and a word spoken in due season, how good is it!" (Proverbs 15:23). You see someone giving you a word about getting a job is good if you're looking for work, but not if you already have a good job. If someone had given me a word about money during my sickness in 2013, I would not rejected that word, it just would not have been the word I needed in that particular time. My health had now become an issue, and no amount of money could change it, nor could money heal me. I needed a word from the Lord concerning this sickness. The Lord had already positioned me right where I needed to be, in the realm of His Glory, which is the atmosphere of heaven where we are not limited to time and space. But more importantly where we can speak a word over every situation and it has to obey you, I will talk more in detail later in the chapter on "sound waves".

IT'S CRITICAL TO BE IN THE "RIGHT" PLACE

Only God knew that the enemy would literally try to kill me in 2013. After spending time in prayer at the close of 2012, I heard the Lord say the word "GLORY", that would be the theme for the new year of hope and I pray that as you read this book, afterwards you too will have an even greater appreciation for the "Glory of God". I will expound on this more in a later chapter, but please underscore this next statement that I'm about to make, as I lay the foundation of this book. This will help, the GLORY of God is the very atmosphere of heaven. Glory is to heaven what air is to the earth. If you can grasp this concept, then you will understand why it is so important to never take lightly the significance of the GLORY. That is why I emphasize that fact the I was already completely consumed with, covered and enveloped with the Glory before sickness infiltrated my body. Thank you Jesus for strategically placing me in a secret place, the Glory of God. "He that dwelleth in the secret place of the most High shall abide under the shadow of the Almighty", (Psalms 91:1).

I truly believe had I been in any other place, not teaching on the Glory, I would not have survived. It was vital for me to be in the" right place at the right time". "He shall cover thee with his feathers, and under his wings shalt thou trust: his truth shall be thy shield and buckler", (Psalms 91:4).

I WAS BEING STONED

First, allow me to spend a few minutes explaining to you what I mean by "I was being stoned". You see stoning is a principle by which something or someone attacks you with multiple problems, at the same time. By now, if you've been saved for a year or longer, you should have at least grown some. Yes, you are still in the process of becoming, but chances are, you have reached a place in your Christian walk, where you can handle one problem at a time. But we are not built to carry the burden of several major problems at once. "Take therefore no thought for the morrow: for the morrow shall take thought for the things of itself. Sufficient unto the day is the evil thereof", (Matthew 6:34). Little did I know that I had several health issues going on, and I wasn't aware of any of them. Thank God I was in the "right place at the right time," teaching on the GLORY OF GOD.

When it finally registered with me, it was December of 2013. While I lay in the hospital for 5 days, I pondered over my condition, and again prayed to God to reveal to me what is going on with all the sickness this year.

When I thought about the fact that for the first forty-five years of my life, I had been anything but sick. As a matter of fact, before this year I had only been admitted in the hospital two times in my life. But this year, as I began this teaching on the GLORY, I've now been hospitalized eight (8) times so far this year. During most of those visits I was facing life-threatening situations. On one occasion I was transferred from one hospital to another by ambulance.

In January of 2013, I was consumed with the Glory of God. The Glory became my meditation, my conversation, and my message. What was supposed to be a one month teaching as every other year, ended up being a series of six months.

In February of 2013, I was going about ministry as usual, when out of nowhere, I looked in the mirror and saw bruises all over my body from head to toe. Because I did not know the cause of the bruises, and at the time had no pain associated with them, I did what most men do; I ignored them. The devil was trying to kill me, but God wouldn't let it be. I tried to hide the bruises from my wife for as long as I could. But that's difficult when you're married to a God fearing, anointed, spirit-filled, woman of God who is also an intercessor.

LET HER IN...TALK TO HER

I want to interject right here to remind any man reading my book, to stop hiding your health issues from your wife. It's pride and it is a trick of the enemy to destroy you. Trust me, I'm speaking from experience. The reason God gave her to you was for her to be a "helpmeet". She has your best interest at heart. Talk to her, tell her what's going on. She loves you. She only wants to see you get better. Stop believing those lies from the devil that she's trying to boss you around or usurp your authority. She's on your side; talk to her.

BONE OF MY BONE

I am so eternally grateful for my beautiful God fearing wife, Rita. It was through her I initially agreed to go to the doctor and get checked out. I still remember it like it was yesterday. I was lying in bed on a Sunday morning, February 17, 2013. I had now grown accustomed to hiding all the bruises that were showing up, even if it meant rearranging my schedule, taking later showers, whatever I had to do to keep her from seeing the bruises. You see, I thought I was protecting her, so she would not worry or stress. I was still feeling fine. The devil was trying to kill me, but he forgot I had a wife who was an intercessor.

On the morning of February 17, I was caught off guard. Without any warning, she walked into the bedroom while I was still asleep. She woke me up and said God wants me to anoint your entire body, and to confirm it Prophet Lonnie Patterson also called and said to pray over you with a red washcloth. I woke up in awe of God that He loved me enough to overlook my ignorance to get me to the doctor. I told her before she prayed, that there was something I needed to tell her. Then I showed her the bruises that had somehow showed up out of nowhere. She immediately said what I thought she would say "you're going to the doctor this morning". I told her no, I was fine, I have a full schedule, and don't have time to go to the doctor. Of course, she talked me into going to the doctor later that day.

I preached our weekend service, then preached Daddy Leon Thomas funeral (the oldest father of our church), then attended my third service that day as a son of the ministry (Bro Steven Jones) spoke that evening. Now, it was time to as they say to "face the music". Thank God I was teaching on the GLORY OF GOD. It is what has carried us through this very difficult storm.

MY WORLD WAS TURNED UPSIDE DOWN

Finally we made it to the doctor after the third service of the day. Have you ever been so sure of something going in your favor, only to discover that you were wrong, and ended up disappointed? I was so looking forward to the doctor's visit that I called both my daughters and told them to meet my wife and I at the doctor's office. I wanted my two girls to meet this doctor, who I thought a lot of, and wanted them to develop a relationship with him. But the words that came out of his mouth concerning my health almost dropped them to their knees. My big point is, God wants us to trust Him in every single situation, including your health.

We are living in a day and time where it's going to be difficult to stand if you do not have you own personal relationship with the Lord. The doctor did lab work and sent us to the patient room to wait on the results. It seemed like it was taking forever for them to come back with the results of my blood work. Then that knock on the door came that we were waiting on, and then came the doctor.

These were his words: "Mr. Smith, I did your lab work, and when I got the results, I asked the nurse to run them a second time." Then he asked if he could pray for me before he went any further. Me, my wife, my two daughters, and the doctor joined hands as the doctor prayed. He went on to tell me that I have no platelets in my blood, and he didn't understand how I was even walking around and not feeling faint. He went on to say that he needed to have me admitted right now. I told him I wanted a second opinion, that I was going to my personal doctor first thing in the morning. I am convinced now, that the GLORY of GOD had been keeping me alive. I was in the "right place at the right time."

7

THE GLORY SHOWS UP IN A PRAYING CHURCH

How bad do you want the GLORY? I've discovered that people will do everything humanly possible in order to have a good service, except pray. We will hire the most gifted preacher, the most gifted musician, and the most gifted praise leader. We will invest a lot of money in sound equipment, improving the acoustics in a building, and all that's fine. But none of these things will have any eternal value if not coupled with prayer.

I never shall forget how one Wednesday evening, it was time for Bible study at New Destiny. I was standing outside the door along with others because intercessory prayers was still going on. As we stood there waiting to go inside, I overheard one of our members make a statement that blessed my life. She said softly, "this is the most praying church, that I've ever attended." Those are the kind of words you want the members to say, because I have found that the "Glory" of God will always rest on a church when prayer has been deemed a priority.

We have experienced so many miracles at New Destiny and I have to say, it has been because of prayer has been a priority. "And Jesus said unto them, It is written, My house shall be called the house of prayer; but ye have made it a den of thieves," (King James Version, Matthew 21:13).

What is Prayer and why should we pray. First and foremost prayer is simply communicating with God (Jehovah) the only true and living God. Prayer is also the vehicle which allows us to go directly to the father, in Jesus's name. Through the finished work of Christ we are able to go boldly to the throne and make our petitions known. When you really grab hold of how prayer actually works, you will realize there's no need to yell or scream. You pray knowing it is as if you are standing right before a Holy God.

Praying to God, in the name of Jesus using God's Word (scripture) in prayer is the most powerful thing we can do for ourselves and for others. The heart of prayer is the will of our heavenly father. Part of that will is simply coming to Him. He desires us as His children to know Him.

He desires your love, your attention, and your fellowship. He desires a time of communion, an intimate time of personal exchange and evolvement. He also desires to release his will and manifest presence in the earth through prayer. As you pray for your needs as well as the needs of others, you are actually becoming a prayer warrior and an intercessor, just like Jesus was and is today. Jesus was sent to destroy the works of the devil, 1 John 3:8, and we have been given the very same authority in the earth through prayer.

When I read what the Bible tells us in 2 Chronicles, it is crystal clear what brought both the "fire and the Glory." As if that wasn't enough, to climax this holy convocation, the Bible also says God shows up and gives us the methodology to summons him again.

"Now when Solomon had made an end of praying, the fire came down from heaven, and consumed the burnt offering and the sacrifices; and the Glory of the Lord filled the house. And the priests could not enter into the house of the Lord, because the Glory of the Lord had filled the Lord's house," (2 Chronicles 7:1-2).

The fact that Solomon had just finished praying, tells me several things:

WHAT IS PRAYER & WHY DOES PRAY PRAYER BRINGS THE GLORY

1.   Solomon had a relationship with the Lord; if you don't have relationship, or you're not in right standing with the Lord, you cannot pray effectively.

2.   Solomon was able to pray according to the word; in order to pray effectively, we must have knowledge of the Word of God.

3.   Solomon had made it a regular practice of consulting with the Lord, before ministering to the Lord; too often we are so consumed with ministering for God, we don't always make time to minister to the Lord.

FOUNDED UPON PRAYER

In 2007, when we finally realized we could not win, whenever the opponent is God, we surrendered. And even though I knew that God had spoken, I refused to move into ministry without more time before the Lord. I called a 21-day fast to pray and sought the Lord for direction. We stood on Ezra 8:21, "Then I proclaimed a fast there, at the river of Ahava, that we might afflict ourselves before our God, to seek of him a right way for us, and for our little ones, and for all our substance."

The fasting and prayer in Ezra 8 is specifically for direction, which was what I needed at that time. If you are in a hard place, and seeking direction, try meditating on Ezra 8.

SACRIFICIAL PRAYER

I feel compelled to share this with you for several different reasons that come to mind, but for one reason in particular. I have so many people even leaders and pastors who have approached my wife and I over the years, with questions like what are you all doing to attract so many people. We always respond the same way because people may see what God is doing in your life or ministry, but fail to understand why. What God is manifesting openly at New Destiny is a direct reflection of the sacrifices we made during the night. Not only did we spend time in prayer and fasting before launching the ministry, but we also made a sacrifice for the Lord. We spent the first year of our ministry in prayer at three o'clock in the morning.

You may be asking why did we do that. My response is as I stated earlier. As the pastor, I refuse to give God that which cost me nothing. There are so many people who say they want the blessings of God but they want ministry to be convenient. It does not work that way. God is looking at our hearts, and our motives, and the attitude in which we do ministry. God himself made a sacrifice, even Jesus was willing to make a sacrifice to disrobe and dishonor himself for us. The Hebrew writer tell us he endured hardship and ridicule for us.

"Looking unto Jesus the author and finisher of our faith; who for the joy that was set before him endured the cross, despising the shame, and is set down at the right hand of the throne of God. For consider him that endured such contradiction of sinners against himself, lest ye be wearied and faint in your minds," (Hebrews 12:2-3).

INTERCESSORY PRAYER

Part of my testimony is that I am alive today, because of intercessory prayer. I know we are accustomed to hearing that Jesus has sat down, and he is no longer working in any shape or form, but I beg to differ with that. The one thing that Jesus will never stop doing is interceding for the church, his bride, the ones for whom he suffered, bled and died.

Look at what the scripture says about Him. "Who is he that condemneth? It is Christ that died, yea rather, that is risen again, who is even at the right hand of God, who also maketh intercession for us," (Romans 8:34). Because I Pastor a church where we have a lot of new believers, therefore I find myself being somewhat redundant sometimes but I want to be absolutely clear what it means to intercede. To intercede, especially if you are in an intercessory prayer meeting, it is vital to understand that you are there to pray for others.

Intercessory prayer has become a part of our weekend service, it sets the tone for the service, and it is what informs us where He is for the service that particular day. There are times when my sermon will change after intercessory prayer because it is clear that God wants to shift to another word. There is never a time when we have a service without intercessory prayer taking place first, at our local church. The flow of the service seems to be off if I visit a place and have to minister in a setting without intercessory prayer.

CORPORATE PRAYER

Corporate prayer is also a regular part of our service every Sunday. I still hold some things dear to my heart, and corporate prayer is one of them. There's just something about bringing the entire church to the altar, grasping and holding one another's hands; praying corporately, together for the various needs of the congregation.

We are so very blessed to pastor a church and lead a congregation that absolutely loves prayer. I have now become accustomed to telling any guest pastor or speaker, unless you're serious about praying, don't call for a prayer line in our church, because our people love to pray, they love to be prayed for. We have made prayer a priority at New Destiny, and it is wonderful!

5AM MORNING GLORY PRAYER CALL

Morning Glory Prayer Conference Call was birthed and established out of my time of sickness in 2013. As many of you know I was hit very hard this year, and the enemy literally tried to take me out, and by all accounts, I'm not supposed to be here. I was diagnosed in February with a very rare blood disease called Thrombocytopenia (ITP) and nearly died because we didn't know how to treat it and our local hospital had never had an (ITP) patient before myself. It was then that our intercessors established the 5AM Prayer Call, as a way to collectively pray for their pastor as well as others.

Since then I've been hospitalized numerous times for various reasons. But the church, New Destiny as well as others began to do what they do best, get in touch with God by way of prayer and communion with God. We are living in treacherous and perilous times, and anyone who does not have their own personal prayer life will not survive the difficult days ahead. Prayer must become a priority in the lives of the believers.

You're invited to join us every Monday, Wednesday, and Friday at 5:00 a.m., and every Sunday evening at 6:00 p.m. – PHONE: 1(605) 475-4700 PIN: 874701

21-DAY DANIEL FAST & PRAYER

One of the things I'm most enthused about is that since the birth of New Destiny, we have establish the fact that we will began each New Year on a 21-Day Daniel Fast. It has grown so much that other church members around our city from other churches now fast along with us for 21-days. We make serving God exciting as it should be. We post our goals and objectives and prayer focus on the social media for others to join in if they like.

I implemented the 21-Day Daniel Fast upon the realization of what Jesus told his disciples when He learned they were unable to cast out an evil spirit. Jesus told them without any hesitation that there are some things that will never be conquered without fasting and prayer. "Howbeit this kind goeth not out but by prayer and fasting," (Matthew 17:21). So you see fasting has now become a way of life for many.

OBJECTIVE: The overall objective of why we fast is always to grow closer to God, to have a more intimate and personal relationship with Jesus Christ. That we may be always lead of the Holy Spirit, and that we will spend more time reading and sharing God's word. And that the Lord will help us turn totally and completely away from all types of sin and rebellion.

WHAT PRAYER DOES FOR BELIEVERS

1. PRAYER GIVES US POWER OVER SPIRITS OF DIVINATION. "And this did she many days. But Paul, being grieved, turned and said to the spirit, I command thee in the name of Jesus Christ to come out of her. And he came out her the same hour," (Acts 16:18).

2. PRAYER HELPS US TO BELIEVE IN OUR DARKEST HOURS. "And at midnight Paul and Silas prayed, and sang praises unto God: and the prisoners heard them," (Acts 16:25).

3. PRAYER GIVES US POWER TO LAY HANDS ON THE SICK. "Is any sick among you? Let him call for the elders of the church; and let them pray over him, anointing him with oil in the name of the Lord," (James 5:14).

4. PRAYER OPENS THE DOOR FOR MIRACLES TO TAKE PLACE. "Then they took away the stone from the place where the dead was laid. And Jesus lifted up his eyes, and said, Father, I thank thee that thou hast heard me (John 11:41).

"GOD WORKS THROUGH SURGEONS HANDS, AND THE DAY I PERFORMED HIS SURGERY, GOD WAS WITH ME 100%."
DR. DANIEL MILLER,
WELLSTAR MEDICAL
CHIEF THORACIC SURGEON

8

FEAR CANNOT REIGN IN THE GLORY

I wish I could tell you that I've gone through all this sickness and pain without ever having to deal with fear. But that's just not the case. To be honest with you, there were many days and nights that fear crept in and tried to setup strongholds in my mind. I had to constantly remind myself of the Word of God which says, "God has not given me a spirit of fear, but a spirit of power, love, and a sound mind," (2 Timothy 1:7).

As a means to understand the essence of this vigorous subject, we must first explore the meaning of this simple four letter word that seems so hard to overcome. I used the phrase "seems so hard to overcome" due to the false illusion that fear is a tangible device or mechanism that we can never revise or train our minds to know that we can conquer. When most people think of fear, they are simply examining the things that cause uneasy feelings that something isn't right or something bad is going to happen. Fear, according the dictionary, has a two-part meaning. One is the agitated feeling caused by anticipation or the realization of danger; and the other is an uneasy feeling that something may happen contrary to one's hopes. But what happens when we are in the Glory of God? Is fear relevant or can it even exist in this type of atmosphere?

We already have an understanding that being in the Glory of God is being in His presence. Any and everything is possible in those very moments when experiencing being in the Glory of God. So where does feelings of doubt or uncertainty have room to rest? The answer to that question is: in our minds. See the key here is God did not give us a spirit of fear, but of peace, love and a sound mind. When we give up these gifts of freedom that the Lord has given us, we open our spirits and minds up for anything to go wrong. Fear can cause a person to miss their mark with God. God's word says we are already blessed, but if there is something that we want we should seek Him for it. So what happens when you are seeking God for a blessing and you miss it due to fear?

Fear can possess many bounding states: killing dreams daily, rendering people powerless, and causing identity crisis, and other things as well. The real issue at hand is not having a clear understanding of fear and the effects it has on our lives. Let's explore fear and the disadvantages it can have in our lives.

Dreams are what drive motivated individuals to get up and make things happen for themselves and their families. Everybody has dreams and goals, but the question is "what is standing in the way of achieving those dreams and goals?" Yes, it could be a number of things but ultimately it usually boils down to being afraid. In this illustration we will see the second explanation of fear.

When we allow our minds to think negative things and ponder on them we begin to doubt and second guess God's strength and ability to make things happen. Not even just strength and ability, but His power to move and change situations. Example: I knew a young lady who was an aspiring poet. She had some absolutely beautiful pieces that were fit for anybody's love song, book, or wherever her imagination would have taken her poetry. She went to an open mic night where the host had invited her to perform one of her poems. She agreed at first, but when entering the establishment to perform, "the dream killer", fear set in and she tried to back out of it.

She started comparing her look to everyone else. She started comparing their work and putting her work down. She was so afraid to perform for several different reasons. One reason was she was amongst her peers. She had experienced hearing negative things pertaining to other people's lives and didn't want anyone to say anything bad about what she was trying to do. Now the thing that I failed to mention is that this young lady would pray before writing, so her pieces were already anointed and priceless. So this young lady continued to battle, in her mind, whether she should perform or not. She began to pray about the situation. The prayer spoken was, "Lord, if this is for me to do, will You let the man come and ask me again?" She needed some reassuring due to her being afraid that things were going to happen contrary to her hopes. The Lord began to work on her right then in that place. There was loud music, people drinking and smoking and God still began to move on her behalf in that place. The young man who was hosting the open mic came to her and stated that he needed her to perform for him.

So she got herself together, prayed and performed her poetry. The introduction that the host gave her was exceptional. The people received her with joy and excitement. The host invited her to a number of events and other avenues in the writing field became available for her as well. Though she never did another open mic, that night taught her something. If you allow fear to rule over you, you will never accomplish anything.

Fear is not the author, nor the finisher of any person's life, BUT GOD IS! Should fear have the ability to kill your dreams, when it is not the reason for the vision in the first place? See we as individuals give power and authority to things over our life that is irrelevant and has no meaning.

The Lord says in Psalm 46:1-2a, "God is our refuge and strength, a very present help in trouble. Therefore we will not fear though the earth gives way." This gives me hope in itself. The Lord just told me He is my PRESENT help. I looked up the word present because I wanted to get a more in depth understanding of the type of help the Lord is providing for me. The dictionary stated that present means now, going on, not past or future; denoting a tense or verb form that expresses a current state or action! That's something to shout about right there. I don't have to wait for God's help, it's already here! Glory to God!

Just think about it for a second. In what way has fear distracted or detoured you from your dreams? Does fear really have that much authority over your life? It shouldn't! It depends on your way of thinking and processing information. What type of mindset do you have? Are you a carnal-minded Christian or a spiritual-minded Christian? When situation and circumstances present themselves to you, does fear overwhelm you or consume you because your mental stability waivers? Or is it your faith? When dealing with issues of being fearful many things play a major role in the outcome of your circumstance.

POWERLESS IN FEAR

Nevertheless, when we allow fear to take control of our minds we are rendered powerless. Imagine, it is pitch black outside and you have not paid your power bill. You get home and all the lights are out. You have no candles, lanterns or anything to light up your home. You are considered without power-in the natural. Let's look at powerless in the spiritual.

Fear drains the very power source that you have twenty four hour access to, and that is God himself. When we encounter fearful or frightening situations we may stop and pray really hard for God to deliver us from whatever it may be at the time. But, because of fear, we challenge God's ability to change or do anything about the situation. It's like saying, "I don't trust that you can get this done any better than I can."

Who are we to challenge God or His motives? The saying "false evidence appearing real" is really a great association with the way we should look at fear. After most fearful encounters, we look back and see that it wasn't as bad as it could have turned out.

Let's look at fear from the first meaning. The first meaning stated fear is an agitated feeling caused by the anticipation or realization of danger. Most people when facing a fearful or dangerous encounter think quickly. Some, depending on the extremity of the matter and according to their mindsets, are not able to control the paralyzing and stagnant physicality's contributed by fear. Can you imagine feeling powerless? You have absolutely no power to move or change the situation at hand.

Paralysis has set in and prevented you from making rational decisions or moves pertaining to your life. Imagine being in a reasonably small area, it's just you and your one year old child. You have what is called arachnophobia-which is the fear of spiders. Your child takes off and is headed straight for a big, brown, hairy spider the size of a ring box. You have never seen this species of spider before, so all sorts of thoughts are racing through your head.

You see the child approaching the spider, but your body becomes like stone as you stand there frozen in your steps. Your mind is telling you, kill the spider before your child gets the spider. All you can do is stand there paralyzed and incapacitated by the presence of an inadequately small creature. The innocent one year old looks back at you with a smile not understanding the immediate danger that you believe is imminent. The spider slowly moves towards your child. You hear and feel the thunderous sound of your heartbeat as if it is about to burst from your very skin.

Though you outweigh this creature by multitudes, you still stand there staring as if you are facing a giant. You call for the child, but the child innocently laughs and continues towards the spider. Finally, someone comes and you beckon for them to kill the spider. You run and grab your child, but you are still shaken from just the presence of this small creature that you fear. Once you have calmed down, you take a look at the dead spider and can't seem to fathom why you are so afraid to pursue killing such a small creature. But nevertheless, even in its death you are still fearful of it.

There are situations and circumstances where there is fear for someone's life. Even in those situations, we should trust and know that the Lord, God Almighty, hear our very prayers and His will shall be done in regards to every aspect of one's life. This is where fear can test your faith. Do you have the faith of a mustard seed? Or do you allow life's challenges to choke the very substance out of the Word that was given to you by the Lord God himself?

It's amazing how fear can have you paralyzed to the place where you are literally at the pleasure of whatever it is you fear. It is not the will of God for us to have fear in anything but Him. So the question arises: "If a person in experiencing the Glory of God, is fear allowed?" It may not be allowed, but it does occur. The difference in the situations is in the Glory of God, being in His presence, you know exactly what to do to overcome your fears. You know what to say and more than likely your first reaction is going to be to pray and recite scripture as a means to conquer the present battle you are facing.

When in the Glory of God, in His presence, this atmosphere is so potent that fear cannot survive in such a powerful environment. The thing that would assist you in overcoming your fears is God's word. The Lord tells us in Hebrews 3:6 so we can confidently say, "The Lord is my helper; I will not fear; what can man do to me?" I don't know about you but I for one am glad to know that the Lord is my helper. And because of this I don't have to be afraid!

FEAR VS. CONFIDENCE

Fear is a case of identity crisis. You have lost confidence and knowledge of who you are and most importantly WHOSE you are. The Lord tells us to be courageous and brave. He tells us to go in confidence. WHOM SHALL WE FEAR? He also says, though an army besieges me, and war break out against me, even then will I be confident. He, God, is letting you know that even in the toughest of situations, to remain confident. He has said on so many occasions that He is our rock and our fortress. He will protect us.

You have to believe the words the Lord is telling you. You have to have confidence and faith in God so that nothing or no one can shake or move the foundation in which the Lord has established within you.

See, I have given examples of situations to help you get a firm understanding of what fear can do to you. Now let me give you substance to help you understand the importance of knowing who you are in Christ and an understanding as to how being in the Glory of God that fear has no authority nor any place to reign.

Confidence is a major, major entity in getting over your fears. You have to have confidence in yourself, through Christ Jesus. Well how do I do that you say. I am not saying it is easy at all. It took a lot of prayer, meditating on God's Word, and a lot of faith to get to that place. But to experience the Glory of God is like having your own personal body guard that you may not be able to see but you can definitely feel God's very presence surrounding you.

We pray for a hedge of protection about us, but that is like a totally different feeling. Take the most dangerous situation you can think of, and know that in the Glory you don't have to fear even in the scariest capacity of one's imagination. The greatest part about this is that when in the Glory, you don't have to worry about what scripture to use for what situation. God will reveal it to you.

It has been my experience to have a prayer come to mind and say Lord, I know this may not be scripture but I need you to hear this prayer. And God directed me to a scripture almost verbatim of what I was praying. Who can know God? Our little minds aren't big enough to fathom the great imagination and wondrous works that He can do. So why put limitations on God by letting fear pressure you to doubt Him? Why should your faith waiver because your confidence level plummeted due to you allowing someone or something to question the very foundation that you know for a fact can't be moved or touched? The very thing that is shaking one's confidence and faith is the very thing that have total control over you at that moment in time. When you lose confidence in knowing that, IF IT'S GOD'S WILL, He will do it, you have nothing left to stand on.

Being in God's Glory is a personal experience that EVERYBODY should want to experience. It is so much peace in an atmosphere where God has taken total control. God has the ability to make your worst nightmare your best blessing ever. Confidence through Christ Jesus is reassuring yourself that you are God's child and you know that all things are possible with God. God is the one and only true God. If God is for us who can be against us? God is the author and finisher of our lives. So, the next time you have a fearful encounter, stop, take a breath, pray and move out the way for God to do His works. The Bible says in everything to go to God with prayer and petition and that we should pray without ceasing. So if you are constantly praying and believing God for whatever it is you are praying about, why is there doubt and fear?

Another thing that the Lord has placed on my heart is, stop making His no's a yes to fit your plans and then get upset when it doesn't come to pass. That is another reason people are afraid to move forward with different things due to being hurt by rejection. I know that may be off subject a little here but that was just placed on my heart to write. I feel the spirit of the Lord saying people get hurt from situations and circumstances because He has given them a firm NO and they continue on with what they want to do instead of taking heed to His instructions. Notice I put in all caps "IF IT'S GOD'S WILL". People, we have got to get to that place where we go before the Lord and plead our cause and WAIT on His answer.

My God, it is my wish that every person will have a chance to be graced by the presence of God in this magnitude. It is not only fear that is ruled out but anything you can possibly think of. God will never leave you nor forsake you. And He means just that.

I know personally of a young woman who had a wonderful opportunity to be able to be in the Glory of God. You could tell because His glory was all over her. It was in her walk, her talk, her confidence and she was truly serving and worshipping God in spirit and in truth. The Lord was truly with her. She was evicted from her apartment but God didn't allow the people to move on the eviction until He provided a place for her to go. I already know that you are looking at the negative portion of this statement. It is not contrary to the human eye to find negativity in all occasions. But the point of this testimony is, who has been evicted and not been thrown out in thirty days? She was allowed to continue staying there for four additional months. That is God! When we just surrender ourselves and move out of the way you will be ecstatic at how awesome God is. Can somebody say GLORY? Thank you Jesus!

Don't let fear question the very heart of God. God wants to bless you more abundantly. I beseech you brothers and sisters, do not allow fear of anything to consume you and your thoughts to where you begin to question God's ability. Remember, nothing is too hard for God. Nothing is impossible for God. The same God that Daniel served, David served, Jesus served and cried out to, is the same God we serve today.

The question is "Do you know who you are?" Or, again most importantly "Do you know Whose You are?" Whom Shall I FEAR? When you know whose you are, everything else is irrelevant. See, the only thing man can do is kill the body. But God, after the killing of the body has a heaven or hell to place you. Another thought crossed my mind after carefully examining the above mentioned incident with the spider:

Oftentimes, men fear other men more so than they do God. It has been documented of the past how man has become corrupt and rebel against God. In what way is this logical? I'm not saying that you should not move out of your bed without asking the Lord's permission, what I am doing is making a plea here for you to fully get an understanding of how we fear the wrong things!

When speaking with a saint it was mentioned that before they were saved they were afraid to do certain things for the fear of angering God. It was stated that after being saved, they felt more at liberty and ease with doing certain things. Saints, I'm here to inform you, do not be deceived with thoughts that after being saved your work is complete. Do not believe the trick of the enemy (Satan), that once saved you can continue to sin and just go to God and say forgive me with no effort or mind to change the matter at hand.

People perish for the lack of knowledge. If there was ever one to fear, it better be God. I don't know about you but I am not looking forward to the fiery lake. It is not my goal to spend all eternity in a burning hell. It is not my wish for my brothers and sisters to spend all eternity in hell. People, God is waiting on us to make a decision to choose him. Yet we choose EVERY THING else. People worshipping gods that cannot save or deliver them.

I know grammatically that these two words that are capitalized are supposed to join as one, but I need you to see a visual of what I am speaking of. We choose EVERY THING over our God who can do multitudes of things. Yet we worship idols that has the power or ability to move NO THING. They can't even move themselves from one place to another. Funny how some people's god can't even move themselves from the living room to the kitchen, but Glory to God, our God is EVERYWHERE!!!! So other than God, who or what is there to fear? Nothing!

NOTHING TO FEAR BUT FEAR ITSELF

When there is substance present, there is no way fear can rest within. Substance in this cause is speaking of spiritual food, God's word to stand on. The only one to fear as mentioned in the above section is God. Other than that there is nothing to fear but fear itself. We have read examples of situations where people have allowed a figment of their imagination to refrain them from pursuing lifelong dreams. Also, the situation about the child and the spider, how simple things can become major things when fear sets in. What if I told you the only person standing in your way is YOU?

Would you be more confident in God's ability to make the things that He has promised you come to pass? For your sake, seek ye the kingdom of God, and all other things will come. You will possess the best gift ever, and that is the firm knowledge of the presence of Almighty God. Fall in love with Jesus. Allow Him to do what he is on the throne to do. Let Him intercede for you without you going back saying – never mind I'm too afraid that you are not going to answer this in the manner that I want it answered.

Again, who are you to challenge the ability, strength and knowledge of God? People we have got to get to a place where God is the absolute love and head of our life. I'm telling you there is no better feeling than to know that God is on your side. That He has your back and will never leave you hanging.

Ask yourself "What is Fear?" In both aspects of the literary meaning of fear it stated that it is a feeling. Try a little exercise: The same energy you put into being afraid, use it to move forward in the Lord. Instead of allowing it to stop you and cause you to become stagnant; allow it to help you trust in God more. Allow it to cause you to stop and believe that not by your might but God's. Allow it to pressure you into a prayer that is so powerful that the frequency and sound waves from your voice destroy demonic holds and assignments in your future. I'm going to leave you with a prayer:

Dear Heavenly Father, I come to you today not on my behalf but on the behalf of my brothers and sisters who are struggling with fear. Father, I know it is not your will for us to allow fear to come in and destroy the very foundation that you have established in our lives. I know that it is not your will for us to face situations that will cause our faith and confidence to waiver. So I'm asking you on their behalf to transform their mind and their mindsets. Help them to come to you when doubt knocks on the door. Help them to tune in to Your frequency so they can hear what the spirit of the Lord is saying pertaining to their lives.

Heavenly Father, let your will be done and not that of our own. Help us to move out of the way and allow you to do what you do best. Father, help your children to know that there is no greater love than what you have shown us. It is my wish that we all experience your glory. Help us to get to that glorious place in you where your presence is evident in our lives.

Heavenly Father, in all things, let it be done that your name is glorified in the highest. Let your light shine in our lives daily. Let your will be done here on earth as it is in heaven. Give us daily bread to live on and live by. Show us continuously how to apply your word to our life.

Heavenly Father, we need you more than life itself. Be our light, Be our guide. Lead us, oh Lord, in Your righteousness. Make your way straight before us. Let us not shame your name in anything we do Father. Deliver our souls, Father, for your name sake.

Help us to not stray. Help us to look to you where our help comes from. Father, search us and know our hearts. Try us and know our hearts and see if there be any wicked way in us and lead us in the way of righteousness.

Father, every hand that so much as touch this book bless them a hundred fold. Give them the in-depth knowledge, wisdom and understanding that they are searching for in you. Help them to understand your greatness beyond materialistic things. Help your people to understand you. Help them to see you for who you are. Help them to understand that there is truly nothing too hard for you nor anything too big for you.

Father help us to understand that your grace is truly sufficient for us. That your love is truly unconditional and greater than any love a man or woman can give. Father, whatever situations or hindrances that is causing your people to become stagnant, give them strength, confidence, courage and zeal to move forward knowing that You are Almighty God and even when we feel like we are alone, we are not alone, for You are with us always.

Father I love you and I ask that you would give every saint one of those comforting hugs you gave me in my time of sorrow. That hug that made me feel like I was the most important person in the world and was loved more than my heart could handle. Father, I know you are merciful and gracious. You are magnificent in all your ways. I wouldn't choose another God if I had a choice. I would choose you every time!!!

I love you, I love you, and I love you some more! It is these things I pray in your mighty son Jesus's name according to your word that states in John 14:13-14, "If I pray and ask in Jesus name, so the Son can continue to glorify the Father, He will do it." Father, your people need you. Cleanse us, purify us, purge us, and make us white as snow. Help us to know you. Let us live in your presence! In Jesus name I pray. Amen.

To the saints: Be blessed in your coming and going. Know that God is not a man that he should lie neither the son of man that he should repent. Know that if He brings you to it, He can and will bring you through it. Put your trust and faith in the Lord God Almighty. I tell you there is truly none like Him. I beseech you to get to know him. Tell him to show you His face. Once you have entered into that arena, I promise you, you will never be the same. You won't look at life the same. Problems and issues just won't be the same. It's like the song say, You won't leave here the same way you came! Learn to enjoy the Lord! I love you and be blessed a million times.

"WHAT I TAKE FROM THIS EXPERIENCE WITH MR. SMITH, IS THAT, IF YOU HAVE FAITH, THEN ANYTHING IS POSSIBLE"

DR. UMA BORATE
HEMATOLOGIST, UAB MEDICINE

9

"THERE'S A MIRACLE IN YOUR MOUTH"

I was in the hospital in November for the eighth time in 2013, and received a WORD in season. The Bible says, "A word spoken in due season, how sweet it is,"(King James Version, Proverbs 15:23). As I laid there in that hospital bed, again, this time in isolation due to Staph infection, the phone call was from my pastor, Dr. R.A. Vernon. He had taken the time to call in between flights to see how I was doing.

After giving him an update on my health condition, he released a WORD over the phone that seemed to have stuck with me since our conversation. He said to me, "Man, I don't know what all God is up to, but one thing I do know is, there is a miracle in your mouth, and I can't wait to see it." And after I handed the phone to my wife to hang up, I lay back down on the hospital bed and I began to meditate on those words spoken to me by Dr. Vernon. "There's a miracle in your mouth, and I can't wait to SEE it."

Whenever the father is speaking to the son, there is an impartation being made. There is something being released from the father to the son. Notice, he did not say, I can't wait to hear it, he said I can't wait to SEE it.

For the miracle in my mouth to be seen, it has to be released from my mouth and into the atmosphere to create a sound wave which has creative power to change my situation. Now it was up to me to take that word and apply it to my situation.

EVERYTHING HAS THE POTENTIAL TO RESPOND

There has been much deliberation on the topic of sound or more importantly sound waves, its role in nature and how it affects mankind. To understand this powerful force God has given us, it is important to split this word to its root as this will facilitate our understanding the power and the purpose of sound waves.

Dictionary.com defines sound in the noun form as: Vibrations that travel through the air or another medium and can be heard when they reach a person's or animal's ear. Wave in its noun form is defined as, (1) A disturbance on the surface of a liquid body, as the sea or a lake, in the form of a moving ridge or swell; (2) A sound wave is defined as a pressure caused by the vibration of something in a medium that transfers energy, like air.

An example of a sound wave would be a burst of loud music through a quiet forest. Notice in defining sound we see that it has the ability to move through air. Air is something that we cannot see with the naked eye. However, we can see the results or air. For example I can turn the air on inside of my home. I cannot see the air itself but objects in the path of air will begin to move. I can see the effects of the air, but not the air itself. Likewise, a wave is something that we cannot see with the naked eye, yet we see the results of a wave. For example, the current in water is created by a wave. In the absence absent of the water we would not have the ability to physically see the wave.

In defining a sound wave, we understand that there is pressure and vibration which produces energy. Energy is also an occurrence that we cannot see. Yet energy is very real. The late German-born physicist Albert Einstein is responsible for the formula that we use to calculate energy today, which is $E = mc^2$. This formula is translated as E [Energy] equals m [Mass] times c^2 [c stands for speed of light]. His research proved although we may not see energy it does exist and is a powerful force.

I would like to add another element that I believe is also important in understanding sound waves and the potential for everything to respond. This element is a molecule. A molecule is defined as the smallest particle of a substance that retains the chemical and physical properties of the substance and that is composed of two or more atoms; a group of like or different atoms held together by chemical forces.

Simply put, molecules make up all living and non-living things. The body is made up of molecules; trees, furniture, and the earth itself are all made up of particles called molecules.

Sound is also a type of wave that we cannot see. Like ocean waves, sound waves need something to travel through like waves through the ocean or through a flag. Sound can travel through air because air is made of molecules. These molecules carry the sound waves by bumping into each other, like dominoes knocking each other over. Sound can travel through anything made of molecules - even water! The speed of sound varies depending on altitude, temperature and the medium through which it travels.

For example, at sea level in a standard atmosphere, at a temperature of 59-degrees Fahrenheit (15 Celsius), sound travels 761 miles per hour (1,225 km/p/h). At a temperature of 32-degrees Fahrenheit (0 Celsius, the speed of sound drops to 742 mph (1,194 km/p/h). In altitudes above sea level the speed of sound is again different and will vary depending on prevailing factors.

The reason for the variations is that sound waves travel by stimulating molecules. When a sound wave hits a molecule it will vibrate, and thereby transfer the vibration to adjoining molecules, which pass it on in a like manner. If molecules are packed very tight, the sound wave can travel very fast, increasing the speed of sound. When molecules are not as densely packed the speed of sound slows.

According to scientist, temperature and altitude affect atmospheric density, changing the speed of sound. Sound will also travel faster through water than through air, because water is a denser medium. Likewise, sound travels faster through steel verses lower-density materials like wood, or atmospheric conditions. For this reason you might see an old movie depicting someone putting an ear to a railroad track to listen for an approaching train, as sound will reach the listener faster through steel rails than by air.

Before we move forward, we have established some things about sound:

- SOUND TRAVELS FASTER IN HIGH TEMPS

- SOUND TRAVELS BY MOLECULES
- SOUND TRAVELS FASTER OVER WATER THAN DRY LAND
- REMEMBER THE SPEED OF SOUND DEPENDS ON HOW TIGHT THE MOLECULES ARE PACKED

As we study the word of God we are often puzzled and yet mesmerized by the many miracles that were created just by God the creator speaking. Genesis 1:1-3 states: "In the beginning God created the heaven and earth. And the earth was without form, and void: and darkness was upon the face of the deep. And the Spirit of God moved upon the face of the water. And God said Let there be light: and there was light."

In these scriptures we see the spirit of God. The written word of God demonstrates the creative power of the spoken word of God. We must come to understand that truly "Life and death are in the power of the tongue and they that love it shall eat the fruit thereof," (Proverbs 18:21).

When we speak we are producing something. What we are speaking determines what is being produced. If I speak negative words, my fruit will be of that negative stock. However, if I speak life into the atmosphere the stock thereof will be life.

This is why I believe it's important not to rehearse the lies the enemy tries to infiltrate our minds with. There is power in the words that are spoken; because once they are released a harvest is being created. The scripture does not say God thought it into existence, but rather he spoke it into existence. Sometimes we must walk through our homes declaring the word of the Lord, on our jobs we must shift the atmosphere by declaring the word of the Lord, we must go into the educational institutes of our children speaking life, and the ability to absorb knowledge, we must go into the doctor's office declaring that "by the stripes of Jesus we are healed!"

Everything has the ability to respond to sound! Think of thunder as it is released, it has the ability to shake tall buildings, and we can feel the effects in our bodies. Yet, Jesus spoke (sound) to the storm and told it to be still! SPEAK TO IT! Everything has the ability to respond.

Look at the power of the word! Mark 11:23 states, "For verily I say unto you, That whosoever shall say unto this mountain, Be thou removed, and be thou cast into the sea; and shall not doubt in his heart, but shall believe that those things which he saith shall come to pass; he shall have whatsoever he saith." The word of God spoken coupled with unfeigned faith is literally unstoppable. Faith and the spoken word of God will remove every hindrance and unlock every door. We cannot be moved by what we see, but rather we must be moved by what we believe as it pertains to the word of the Lord. Whatever he has promised he will perform, if we can only believe.

Ps 107:19-20 states, "Then they cry unto the LORD in their trouble, and he saveth them out of their distresses. He sent his word, and healed them, and delivered them from their destructions." How did he send his word? Through sound waves!

These are fractions of the scriptures, helping us to see that speaking the word of God into the atmosphere is powerful. How was it that Jesus was able to speak to a raging sea? Everything has the ability to respond when sound waves are released into the atmosphere.

It is so important to be very careful about what we release by way of sound waves. Jesus spoke to the raging sea and simply told it "Be still!"
We need to walk into some raging situations and simply speak the word of God – "Be still." We should always be careful not to ever speak down to people because remember words are producing. If you tell your son or daughter they will never succeed, they will have a difficult time succeeding because of the words spoken over them.

I personally know two people that lost their parents at an early age. Both would often make statements that they believed they wouldn't live long productive lives. They both believed they would die at an early age as their parent did. Both died at an early age, but they both always spoke death on their lives. They both received the fruit of what they declared.

Everything is nature has the ability to respond to sound. A fetus has the ability to respond to sound. Some scientist believe that by week nine the unborn fetus can react to loud noise. And by the end of the second trimester, the fetus can hear.

Research has shown that when the mother begins to speak the heart rate of the fetus will slow down. This seems to suggest that the fetus recognizes the voice of the mother, which means the unborn child can hear. This is why when a baby is born many times the baby will attempt to turn its head in the direction of the mother or father speaking.

If a baby is exposed to music in-vitro they will generally calm when music is played. Even premature infants, at 24 to 25 weeks, respond to the sounds emitted around it. Many newborn infants enjoy the sound of water. Why? Because inside the mother is the sound of blood traveling through the blood vessels, as well the rumbles of the stomach as food enters and leaves the digestive track. Everything has the ability to respond to sound!

Animals have the ability to respond to sound. The owl is a creature that is thought to have the sharpest hearing. They have very large ear holes which are situated above, below, and behind eye level, depending on the species which allows them to have pinpoint accuracy as to sound. An owl's range of audible sound is not unlike humans, but their hearing is much more acute which allows them to hear the slightest movement. Again everything in nature has the ability to respond to sound.

Because I believe the unadulterated word of God is our best source for understanding the purpose and power of sound waves, I will go back to the scriptures. I simply desire to show through a few other situations that everything can respond to sound. I particularly like Ezekiel 37:1-15, "The hand of the LORD was upon me, and carried me out in the spirit of the Lord, and set me down in the midst of the valley which was full of bones and caused me to pass by them round about: and, behold, there were very many in the open valley; and, lo, they were very dry. And he said unto me, Son of man, can these bones live?"

Notice here again we have "The spirit of the Lord," his Glory! Then the Lord is speaking to the Prophet Ezekiel, "Can these bones live?" Many times in this thing called life, we endure heartaches and pain along the journey. Through this journey, our dreams can seem to die. Some endure sickness in their bodies, some in their mind, divorce, the loss of loved ones, financial difficulties, and the list can go on. We begin to wonder even in our "sanctified minds", can I make it after all of this? The answer is, YES YOU CAN! YOUR BREAKTHROUGH IS IN YOUR MOUTH!

Let's look at the next verse. "And I answered, O Lord GOD, thou knowest. Again he said unto me, prophesy upon these bones, and say unto them, O ye dry bones, hear the word of the LORD. Thus saith the Lord GOD unto these bones; Behold, I will cause breath to enter into you, and ye shall live."

WAIT THIS SOUNDS LIKE

Genesis 2:7-8 says, "And the Lord God formed man of the dust of the ground, and breathed into his nostrils the breath of life; and man became a living soul." GOD BREATHED INTO MAN THE BREATH OF LIFE!

~YE SHALL LIVE!

God is the creator of all things. He causes life to be resurrected unto a person. We will try everything else, but if we just yield ourselves to the Master he will revive, restore, and resurrect everything that has been lost through the storms of life. "And I will lay sinews upon you, and will bring up flesh upon you, and cover you with skin, and put breath in you, and ye shall live: and ye shall know that I am the LORD. So I prophesied as I was commanded: and as I prophesied, there was a noise, and behold a shaking, and the bones came together, bone to his bone. And when I beheld, lo, the sinews and the flesh came up upon them, and the skin covered them above: but there was no breath in them," (Ezekiel 37:6-8).

As the prophet spoke according to the instruction of the Lord, the bones came together. Still there was no life! The prophet was instructed to now prophesy to the four winds to breathe upon the slain that they may live. In other words, SPEAK TO IT!

YOU MUST SPEAK THE WORD OF THE LORD OVER YOUR SITUATION!

Again, it doesn't matter what you are going through, SPEAK THE WORD OF THE LORD over every situation, and watch that situation turn around. There are many voices throughout this land. We have the voice of family, friends, the workplace, television, radio, internet, and the list can go on. However, we need to hear the word of the Lord and speak that word throughout our lives.

Because sound wave is pressure caused by the vibration of something in a medium that transfers energy, sound is not limited to verbal communication. Sound can be created by the clapping of the hands, the patting of one's feet, musical instruments. Sound is also created through the groans of the believers as Romans 8:26 states, "Likewise the Spirit also helpeth our infirmities: for we know not what we should pray for as we ought: but the Spirit itself maketh intercession for us with groaning which cannot be uttered."

I now understand the church mothers who would often hum and groan unto the Lord. Have you ever seen a time when all you could do was just hum or groan, there were simply no words? Could you feel the presence of God? Somewhere between the beginning and the ending you felt a sense of peace literally overtake you overtake you. This is an example of the spirit making intercession with groans! Glory to God!

"I DON'T KNOW THE PURPOSE OF ALL THE SICKNESS YOU'RE GOING THROUGH, BUT I KNOW ONE THING, THERE'S A MIRACLE IN YOUR MOUTH, AND I CANT WAIT TO SEE IT"

-Dr. R A Vernon

10

GOD HAS A PLAN

My sickness may have caught me by surprise, but certainly not God. You see, God always has a plan. In the previous chapter we dealt with sound waves and the fact that everything has the potential to respond to sound. In this chapter we will unravel the idea that our situations though they may seem helpless and hopeless are working for YOUR GOOD and GOD'S GLORY!

All at the same time. The scripture emphatically declares that " ALL THINGS work together for the good to them that love God, to them who are the called according to his purpose," (King James Version, Romans 8:28). It doesn't matter what is going on with or around you, if you love God and have aligned according to HIS purpose then whatever your situation, it is working for your good and his GLORY!

Before our very existence God had a divine plan and purpose in place for us. Creation itself speaks to this very fact. The very fact that you and I exist today is a testament to God having a plan. According to scientist, typically a female is born with millions of immature eggs that are anxiously waiting the times of ovulation. The key words are: "there are literally

67

millions of eggs waiting!" I don't know anyone that has a million children, so that means all the eggs do not fertilize. So in understanding this fact we understand that only a few unfertilized eggs make it through to become fertilized.

I am amazed that there were millions of eggs waiting, yet I made it! Just meditate on that for just a moment. You made it! I made it! God has a purpose and a plan for your life. I feel it necessary to say this, it doesn't matter if you were the product of unwed parents, rape, attempted abortion, neglect, whatever the situation, GOD HAS A DIVINE PURPOSE AND PLAN FOR YOUR LIFE!

Sometimes there are circumstances beyond our control that surround our birth. The evil one will attempt to use those circumstances to make you feel that you were a mistake. I tear that down and bind it in the name of Jesus! You were not a mistake, but rather God has a purpose and a plan for your life! God will strategically use these situations to be elevators in your life. Every valley that I have walked through in life gave me the ability to encourage and pray someone else through, WHY? Because I could identify with their pain!

First, however we must allow the Lord to deliver us, or as he told Simon: "And the Lord said, Simon, Simon, behold, Satan hath desired to have you, that he may sift you as wheat: But I have prayed for thee, that thy faith fail not: and when thou art converted, strengthen thy brethren," (Luke 22:31-32). Once Simon was converted he could then go back and strengthen, "help establish", his brethren. Once we have first received deliverance and healing in those parts of our life then we can go back and strengthen and help establish our brethren.

Jeremiah 29:11 states, "For I know the thoughts that I think toward you, saith the Lord, thoughts of peace, and not of evil, to give you an expected end." Let us closely examine this scripture as we grow to understand that our situation will give God Glory. The children of Israel now find themselves in a place of bondage. The Lord says for seventy years they would be in this pagan land, but he gave them instructions – plant, build, buy, be productive in this land because if there is peace in the land you will have peace.

"This is what the Lord Almighty the God of Israel, says to all those I carried into exile from Jerusalem to Babylon: Build houses and settle down; plant gardens and eat what they produce. Marry and have sons and daughters; find wives for your sons and give your daughters in marriage, so that they too may have sons and daughters. Increase in number there; do not decrease. Also, seek the peace and prosperity of the city to which I have carried you into exile. Pray to the Lord for it, because if it prospers, you too will prosper...!"(New International Version, Jeremiah 29:4-7).

Although they had to endure being away from their home for a season, they would return back to their homeland. They could have used this time to complain. "Why?" But instead they obeyed the voice of God. He instructed them that if they obeyed they would enter back in their land with substance. Although their disobedience caused them to be in this place of bondage, God had a plan to bring them out!

He didn't just bring them out, they came out with SUBSTANCE! When you have endured the trials of life make sure you come out of it with the spoil from the trial! That's exactly what David did when he fought against Goliath.

Goliath had defied the army of the living God. But notice David, who had been on the backside of the mountain caring for the sheep, and would eventually serve as Israel's next King, "And Samuel said unto Jesse, are here all thy children? And he said there remaineth yet the youngest, and, behold, he keepeth the sheep. And Samuel said unto Jesse, send and fetch him: for we will not sit down till he cone hither,"(King James Version, 1 Samuel 16:1).

David was in training for his next move in God, regardless of the fact that he was caring for the sheep, God was going to get Glory out of the situation. "Then Samuel took the horn of oil, and anointed him in the midst of his brethren: and the Spirit of the Lord came upon David from that day forward So Samuel rose up, and went to Ramah," (1 Samuel 16:13).

God had a divine purpose and plan for David! Don't allow your now to rob you of your next! "And David spake to the men that stood by him, saying, What shall be done to the man that killeth this Philistine, and taketh away the reproach from Israel? For who is this uncircumcised Philistine, that he should defy the armies of the living God? And David said unto Saul, Thy servant kept his father's sheep, and there came a lion, and a bear, and took a lamb out of the flock, And I went after him and smote him, and delivered it out of his mouth: and when he arose against me, I caught him by his beard, and smote him, and slew him," (1 Samuel 17:26; 34-35).

Someone the people did not think was capable of bringing victory, but God always has a plan for his people. It is our responsibility to just simply obey him and move at his leading. Many times we can't figure it out, we must "faith it out!" David told Saul the same God that gave me the victory with the lion and the bear is the same God that would give him the victory with Goliath. David didn't use the usual armor, instead he told Goliath: "I COME TO THEE IN THE NAME OF THE LORD OF HOSTS, THE GOD OF THE ARMIES OF ISRAEL..."(I Samuel 17:45).

Goliath was defeated that day and all that belonged to Goliath was delivered unto Israel. "And the children of Israel returned from chasing after the Philistines, and they spoiled their tents," (I Samuel 17:53). Go in the battle knowing that in Jesus we are already victorious; he has already gotten the victory! Therefore, come out with all of the spoil of the evil one. This is a testament to the undeniable Glory of God! If God is for you, it doesn't matter who situates themselves against you! It is all to the Glory and honor of God!

What was meant to destroy you now becomes a platform to help others to come through the pain of whatever they have endured. One of the greatest depictions of this is found in 2 Corinthians 4:7; 17: "But we have this treasure in earthen vessels, that the excellency of the power may be of God, not of us. For our light affliction, which is but for a moment, worketh for us a more exceeding and eternal weight of Glory!"

The Apostle Paul was in great conflict. But conflict loses its power in the matchless Glory of God! When we understand that our light affliction is truly working in us "a more exceeding weight of Glory" we will view our conflicts much differently.

The Apostle Paul knew the power of God to the degree that he was content no matter what the circumstances were. Going through the fire of life will teach you to stand in spite of circumstances.

The Apostle had staying power, enduring power, he stood firm on the word of God. He knew God as faithful, he knew God as "the God of Glory." Nothing is too hard for God! We must trust God to the degree that despite what our physical eyes see, our faith says God has a plan! And he is getting the Glory out of my situation. We must have enduring power as well as some staying power.

Although the Apostle Paul wrote much of the New Testament, he was human and he could feel the various obstacles that must be endured. God wants to make visible the truth of the gospel, this happens when we allow the Glory of God to shine through our circumstances. If this truth, this gospel be hidden, it is hidden to those that are lost. There is a plot by the kingdom of darkness to keep the body of Christ in darkness! But it will not avail, "Arise, shine, for thy light is come, and the Glory of the Lord is risen upon thee. For, behold, the darkness shall cover the earth, and gross darkness the people: but the Lord shalt arise upon thee, and His Glory shall be seen upon thee," (Isaiah 60:1-2). When gross darkness is present the Glory of the Lord shows up!

Anywhere there is light darkness must flee. I would like to share a few testimonies of people that have stayed the course. It looked like they would never come through but they came to realize God had a plan. For the sake of their privacy I will not use their names, but these are true stories.

Lady 1 - At an early age she was exposed to the spirit called rejection, as her father rejected her as a child. Although his family accepted and acknowledged her; he never accepted her as his daughter. She often felt that she was a misfit, or as she states "the black sheep" of her family. Her other siblings had a relationship with their father.

Her mother was in college when she became pregnant with "Lady 1". Subsequently, there were times when her mother say that she had to drop out of college because of her pregnancy. This also made "Lady 1" feel guilty. Even though her mother's statements weren't meant to hurt her, they did.

As she grew up, she would try to compensate for this empty place in her heart. As a teenager she became involved in an intense relationship but after some time the relationship ended. Devastated, she turned to drugs to numb the pain. The more she engaged in this behavior everything around her began to crumble. She felt more and more rejected because her family was responding to her actions verses her pain or what I call "soul wound."

Now looking at this story one would think this is a downward spiral. However, at her lowest point, while high on drugs, she stated she heard the devil say he was going to kill her! BUT GOD HAD A PLAN! She called her family and told them she needed help. She was admitted into treatment, and although she gave up, God never gave up. As a matter of fact GOD HAD A PLAN FOR HER LIFE!

God always has outstretched hands for his children. She has been clean now for fifteen years, and she counsels other young ladies through all manner of addictions. I would firmly say God is getting Glory out of this situation!

Man 1 - He grew up in a God fearing family. His Father was a pastor and his mother a first lady. He grew up in a middle class family, where there was a strong emphasis on family, education, and serving God. He was successful in just about everything that he attempted. So many times he had to search for things that were a challenge. He was often told by the Church mothers "God has a call on your life son." That didn't really matter to him, as he stated "God called my dad not me!"

As he grew into adulthood he seemed to be more intrigued with the street life, in spite of his parents attempting to lead him into another direction. Although his parents would press him about his dreams and aspirations, he just didn't seem to be interested. He was very gifted with words, whether citing poetry, writing, or talking. It was very obvious.

At the young age of twenty he began to get involved with the law. It was small things at first, but "it's the small foxes that destroy the vine." Soon the small things became large, until one day his parents received a call that he had been arrested and the charge was "attempted murder."

Now at the age of twenty-two their son was facing "attempted murder" charges, and yes, he did shoot at someone. He had become suicidal before this incident and it is believed that some other elements were the causes of this infraction. However, regardless of those issues it is obvious what is really behind all of it. The enemy comes to steal, kill, and destroy! By any means necessary.

The State took this case against this young man and attempted to give him life in prison. BUT GOD HAD A PLAN! After much prayer, God turned the situation around and the young man was given ten years in prison. He did ten hard years, and at one point he states "I thought I was going to lose my mind in there!" but GOD HAD A PLAN!

He was released after he served those ten years. At first the adjustments were very difficult. He was only twenty-two when he went into the system, now he was thirty two. He had to learn how to function as a free man, but GOD HAD A PLAN!

In prison, he had learned how to call on the name of Jesus. He had learned that all along God had a purpose and a plan for his life. When he couldn't talk to anyone else, he could always talk to God, and he found that God was a friend that was closer than any family member could ever be. He found God to be a provider, a deliverer, a forgiver, a redeemer, a very present help in anytime of trouble.

Today this young man is married, has children, and serves in ministry traveling and talking to other young guys. He says if he can save one young man from traveling down that path it's all worth it.

Man 2 - He grew up in a middle class family that was active in the community, but more importantly, active in the church. He spent every Sunday working at or around the church with his father. However, at the age of nine his parents went through a terrible divorce and it left Man 2 scared and confused. His father moved on and remarried, which made him feel rejected because his father led a busy life and there wasn't much time for Man 2 anymore.

He grew up and attempted to move past the pain of his childhood, but the remembrance would often come back to haunt him. It wasn't long before Man 2 began turning to the streets. Although he had this strong Christian background, he was not married, and had a good job; he was beginning to turn his back on it.

He stated "how could my life be normal one minute and turn to something unrecognizable overnight." As he exclaimed it felt as though his life transitioned to something he didn't recognize at the blink of an eye. Man 2 became bitter with church, his life, and everything around him.

He soon met a young man that introduced him to drugs, he thought why not? So began his journey with crack cocaine. At first this seemed to be a good way to escape all the things he didn't understand. As with any addiction he started out feeling as though he could control it, but there comes a time when the addiction begins to control the person.

He soon came to the point that he couldn't keep a place to live, a job, or any income for any length of time. As soon as he would get paid he would use until all that money was gone. As his addiction progressed, he began to sell items out of his home. His wife became so frustrated that she left. This pushed him further into the addiction.

Most people had lost hope in Man 2. But his mother and siblings faithfully prayed for his deliverance. More importantly, GOD HAD A PLAN FOR HIS LIFE. Man 2 struggled for ten years with his addiction and there were numerous highs and lows. He would go through treatment, come out determined to make a new life only to relapse within a month. He stated "I could get clean, but I had problems staying clean!"

When God has a plan for your life and he is getting Glory from your situation it may look hopeless. This is great ground for the Glory of God to be manifested! It is through these times, when man has exhausted all, God steps in and does for us what we could not do for ourselves! GLORY TO GOD!

After twelve years of ups and downs, treatment centers, and believing God for a breakthrough, he is now sober and expecting his first child. He now works within the system to help other addicts obtain their sobriety. He forgave his father, and he took responsibility for his own actions.

The enemy will use every situation for the demise of the saints, BUT GOD! He has a plan for our lives and our trials are our employees. The trials help us to see the manifested Glory of God in our situations. We must always remember, the greater the storm, the greater the Glory, "For our light affliction, which is but for a moment, worketh for us a far more exceeding and eternal weight of Glory....!"(2 Corinthians 4:17).

All these stories are factual, and while some had given up on them. GOD NEVER GIVES UP! As long as there is life in your body there is that opportunity for true transformation. I want you to know that God has a plan for your life! And he will get the Glory out of every situation!

As Dr. R. A. Vernon states in his book, *Size Does Matter,* "Don't look at where you are right now, keep your vision in front of you and aim. See yourself where you want to be."

11

THERE'S OBEDIENCE IN THE GLORY

OBEDIENCE IS BETTER THAN SACRIFICE

I believe one of the things that lead to frustration, is that sometimes it is hard for us to accept what God has already willed for our lives. In reality, we don't believe that God is able to take care of us as his word claims, which makes it hard for us to obey God. We sing this beautiful song called "I give myself away so you can use me", but little do we know, God is omniscient (all knowing). He knows when we really mean, "I loan myself to you", because we have not reached a place in God, where we can trust him enough to obey him. But even more importantly, it is vital that we obey the Lord when he speaks to us, or gives us a command.

Let me tell you from experience, that God will take care of his children, and that revelation comes with simple obedience. This is a truth that you will never come to know, unless you obey him, and allow God to reveal himself to you as he did Abraham. God was never revealed in scripture as Jehovah Jireh, (The Lord Who Provides) until Abraham stepped out on faith and followed God, even though he had no idea where he was going. But as he left with his only son Isaac, headed up Mount Moriah, God was already preparing his blessing.

By the time they reached the place of worship, "God said to him, now I know I have your heart, and you will do whatever I ask you to do," (Genesis 22: 11-14). It was at that moment in time, for the very first time that God was revealed as Jehovah Jireh. Do you trust God enough to follow him, and believe him, even when don't see any possible way for God to do what he promised you? It is in these types of situations that God is trying to bring you to that place of total dependence upon him.

GOD KNOWS OUR HEART

Don't ever kid yourself into believing that you can fool God. Remember that the manufacturer will always be greater than that which is manufactured. My point here is God made us and he also knows our heart, thoughts, and even our motives behind what we do.

God did not want Israel to have a king first of all, mainly because he wanted to be their everything. Have you ever wanted something that you know you really did not need? This is where God's chosen people got into trouble, and it is also where so many of us get trouble as well. They wanted to be like all the other nations. All the other nations had kings.....so hey....they figured, we need a king too.

Be very careful in trying to fit in with every crowd. Some places you simply don't need to go. Some people you simply don't need to befriend. And there are some things you just don't need to experience, you are better off in the long run without the trouble that comes along with it. But because they wanted a king, God granted it to them, even though he warned them through the prophet Samuel, this would turn out to be a costly mistake. Have you ever gone against what you knew God was saying, but felt you had to do it, or had to have it?

You see there are so many hidden nuggets in the Holy Scriptures. One of those nuggets is the fact that when God speaks of obedience, there is usually some type of blessing that comes along with your obedience. One of the great Bible lessons on obedience is when God had given King Saul specific instructions about destroying ALL the Amalekites, and save nothing alive.

But then the Prophet Samuel comes along and ask the king one simple question, "Did you destroy ALL the Amalekites, both man and beast, and leave nothing alive?", (I Samuel 15: 18-19). And of course, the king lied and said, "Yes, I destroyed everything, just like God said to do", (I Samuel

15:20). It was about that time that one of the sheep blurted out, Bahhhhhhhhh. And when the prophet Samuel responded to him saying "if you destroyed everything, what is this noise in my ear?", (I Samuel 15:14). King Saul answers by saying, "Oh that, you see, the people wanted to save alive some of the best animals", (I Samuel 15:15). But what about what God says? Don't ever allow people to get you in trouble with God.

WHEN WE OBEY HIM, WE SEE HIS GLORY

The Bible teaches us that before we start out on a journey, or to begin a new project, to first sit down, reconcile, and count up the cost. It was only by the grace of God that we obeyed God in 2007, stepped out on faith, started a Church with nothing but a promise from God. We have lifted up the name of JESUS from that day until now although many think it's old fashion. Let me be the first to tell you, if Jesus is not the main attraction, that's not a Church you attend, that's called a get together!

Because I refused to back down from preaching JESUS, and launched a PRAYER CAMPAIGN, The Glory of God began to show up from the first Bible study held in our home in March of 2007. When God speaks to me, he knows me, he made me, he wired me up this way, he knows, it don't have to make sense to me, I just need to know God said it.

After meeting in my home for two weeks, The Lord spoke to me and said move out. So in April, I moved out, with no sound system, no mics, no money, only a few people, mostly family. In April of 2007, we settled in on Rainbow Drive, AL, inside the conference room at Motel 6 which held about fifty people.

I will never forget the first service at Motel 6; I was a nervous wreck. My wife was in her quiet prayerful mode, not doubting, just prayerful. She's always been my biggest supporter. As we are getting dressed, it's quiet in our home. Our children decided to stay at our former church, I so desperately only wanted a confirmation from God. By now my palms are sweating bad.

After we get dressed, it's almost time to walk into the hardest thing we ever had to do. Believe me, it takes a special grace, I say this humbly, to be a founding pastor. Think about it, why would people follow you, when you have absolutely nothing (hoping you will get something, when they can go to the church down the street, which is already established, with children's church, and various ministries already in place. But I felt God hand was on us.

GOD WANTS OBEDIENCE

As we got ready to leave the house for our first service at Motel 6, the phone rang. It was a young lady with whom we had attended high school. She said, I was just calling to check with you all, because I've been hearing rumors......are you all starting a church at Motel 6. We responded by telling her yes we are, and today is the first service. She responded by saying O.K., I'm coming. What time does it start?

It was just what I needed, at the time that I needed it, to boost my faith that God was leading us this way, and it was right on time. I want you to know, that if you Obey God, He will do what He said He would do.

We left home, and if we were not already going through enough, while I left early to set up chairs and get ready for the service. My wife, who came to church a little later gets pulled over by the police on her way to the very first service. Needless to say, it looks like once again, what have I done Lord, I'm trying to support my husband's vision, but it's not starting out the way I thought that it would. But God always allows the devil to throw the first blow, but when we finally got to Motel 6, and started our first service as a church, New Destiny was born.

The young lady who had called that morning had also showed up for that service, along with her sister, cousins, and we had about 40 more people who showed up for the service and also joined. Many times we try to figure out how God will finish the work, but you don't need finishing grace, you need starting Grace. MOVE WITH THE CLOUD! It's vitally important to move when God moves.

The scriptures teach us that Moses moved when the cloud moved. This should teach us to stay hungry for God, and after you discover where He's working join him. It was Henry Blackerby and Claude B. King in their book "Experiencing God", who made the statement, "Anytime you join God where He's working, you will always experience Him."

You see at Quality of Life (QOL), we did not advertise the ministry at all. We were on the backside of the building, with no way for people to visibly see from the highway where we were actually meeting. I mean the only way you could find us, is that you had to be looking for us.

The Lord spoke to me and said don't ever think that you did this, meaning caused this church to GROW. He said, "I did it and don't ever allow anyone to make you think that you did it." God spoke to me and said "If you Go-Low" then I can trust you, and this is only a glimpse of what I will do through you if you "Go-Low" and stay humble, and keep all the focus on ME, saith the Lord.

After eight months we had grown to over 200 members while a QOL. It was time to start looking for another place to hold our service because we were now starting to attract new families, the real harvest which we prayed for from day one. Many of them were looking for a place that could offer children's church, and youth ministry to name a few.

God blessed us to find our own facility within a year's time. These were truly "growing pains", the kind of problems a pastor loves to have. I say this with all humility, the people kept coming and I didn't know where we were going to put them all. After our first year of taking out a loan, God blessed the faithful members of New Destiny to burn the 15 year mortgage within 15 months. It was getting a little crazy by now.

By the third year of ministry we had grown to over 400 members, and we were still praying and seeking God for his directions about ministry, covering, connecting and the whole works. The only thing I knew to do was to "Go-Low" and stay low, because when your ministry is growing people tend to think you have some type of formula, or magic wand. And it was about this time our ministry was starting to make an impact in our city, and I could feel it.

GROWING PAINS

At the rate the ministry was growing, it didn't take a rocket scientist to realize that the enemy is not going to just sit back and allow you to continue to lead people to Christ, to help them to rededicate their lives back to the Lord, without attacking you. It has always been my passion to minister to couples, and my wife and I take great pride in the fact that that we have married nearly forty couples over the last six years. On two occasions I married two couples on the very same day.

Needless to say our ministry was now on hell's hit list. The ministry at this point had seen 800 people walk down the aisles to accept JESUS as their Lord and Savior. We began to have our share of trials and tribulations just like everyone else, but I was determined to stay with what got us here, prayer, preach, teach, and live JESUS. And the Lord kept blessing this young church, and we continued to focused on soul-winning, which we still emphasize today, along with loving people.

I think every pastor probably experience this at some point in ministry, when it seems like, God is not moving as fast as we would like, and just maybe God needs our help, right? Wrong. God is doing it ALL. Our part is simply to OBEY GOD, and watch Him do what seems impossible. At this point, you have to remind yourself of all the promises God made you in the beginning.

It's easy to get caught up in all the distractions that the enemy will bring against you, and if you're not careful, you will find yourself playing right into the hands of the enemy. My sickness was something the devil threw at me, to shake me, to move me from the GLORY. But I want to serve notice on the devil right now, that I shall not be moved, God is looking for obedience, even when it doesn't make sense, trust GOD with your situation.

MAKE SURE YOU ARE CALLED BY GOD

The Bible tells us to make our calling and election SURE. If you have truly been called by God, no matter how tough it may seem...stay in the fight because God is trying to use you to bring Himself Glory. Ministry is not a game, and it is dangerous to be in ministry, and not be called by God. You may be reading this book wondering how can someone preach without being called by God. There are some people who have intruded into the ministry for the wrong reason, and others have mistakenly stepped into the wrong office.

Dr. Vernon made a very profound statement at one of the Gathering of the Shepherd's (GOTS) meetings, that I have found to be true. He said there are some people who WANT to preach, more than they are CALLED to preach. This is so key, because when you are CALLED, God gives you the grace to stand, endure, and go through whatever you have to go through.

You cannot be in ministry because it looks glamorous, or exciting, again you have to be CALLED. Just because you have gifts, talents, and special abilities, that is not a CALLING. Never allow anyone to persuade you to go into ministry, even if your entire family is in ministry.....if you have not been CALLED. I know a man who was an awesome servant in the ministry. He and his family were in regular attendance, actively involved in ministry. He allowed people to persuade him to go into ministry.

Immediately after announcing he had been called to preach, he started taking engagements. The problem with this was, his wife was a new convert who had recently accepted Jesus. My heart still aches for this beautiful family as they are now divorced. I'm not saying he was not called, but I don't think it was the right time. We must know without a doubt that it was God who called us, and move only when God says move!

It is also important to remind yourself, that the enemy would not try to distract you or get you off course if the ministry was not really making an impact for JESUS. It's also important that while the pastor is trying to reach the world, and minister to the masses, that someone is ministering to the pastor, as well as for the pastor, by way of intercession. If not, trust me as humble as He may be, he will be pushed like Moses, to the place of being provoked to strike the ROCK, when God said to speak to the ROCK.

You see the reason God issued such strong punishment on Moses, is because God had placed Moses in a position like He has so many of you ....to bring Him Glory. I want you to read carefully the words God spoke to Moses after Moses struck the rock. Get this..... "Moses, why did you not sanctify me in the eyes of the people?", (Numbers 20:12). In other words, Moses stole some of God's glory, and if you don't get this, then you've missed the whole revelation of the book, God wants to use you to BRING HIM GLORY!

I'm after the souls winner's crown. At this point, we (new Destiny) are weeks away from moving into the new church. I will soon launch the new vision for the family life center. I move with the cloud. I don't have to see the provisions, I believe God. My job is to cast vision before the people. They have bought into the vision. We have labored in the word, taught the people about giving, sowing, tithing, what God expects from his chosen people, who we are as a church, and the most important thing, our assignment in this community.

The people are GROWING SPIRITUALLY.....which is what every pastor wants to see happen in their church, not swelling, not moving from church to church.......but GROWING SPIRITUALLY! This was encouraging to see God allow you to raise up and groom spiritual leaders and help equip them for ministry, ordain them, license them to preach the Gospel, and most of know the spirit that is within those who serve with you in ministry.

Anytime God has plans to use you for his Glory, please understand this, there will be some cost involved, there will be some loss involved, there will be some setbacks, there will be some people leave your life that you thought would be with you forever. I've learned this from my pastor, Dr. Vernon. Never speak derogatory about them, but thank God for the years they served with you in ministry no matter how much it hurts you, speak well of them, they are still saved and love Jesus as much as you do.

I shall never forget the life changing sermon preached by Dr. Vernon...."It Had To Happen". Accept the fact that there are some things in life that must happen to make us better fit for the assignment God has for us. Remember it's not always what you' going through, but many times, it's what you're thinking about what you're going through.

I've learned to get a reversal of my thinking in most every situation. I have learned by now that as a pastor, trying to live holy, being faithful, keeping your hands above the table, Psalms 24 says, "Whom shall ascend unto the hill of the Lord, he that hath clean hands and a pure heart". When the Lord has his hands on you, and has plans to use you, you must prepare yourself and the congregation you lead about spiritual warfare. They must also know that as Paul stated "we wrestle not against flesh and blood, but against principalities and Powers, against the rulers of the darkness, against spiritual wickedness in high places", (Ephesians 6:12). This means that the congregation must also understand what spiritual warfare is all about, that they may be able to recognize when the enemy has gained a foothold in the ministry. If this is left undone, you will pay for it down the road.

GOD WILL HURT YOU TO HELP YOU

There are some things in life that will be discovered the hard way, sometimes it comes through pain. One of things I found out, when I began to chase hard after God with a "Greater Passion" is that to have passion for something, or be passionate about something or someone, you are placing yourself in a position to suffer a bit of pain. Even if that someone is GOD. Let's be clear, in order to have a serious love relationship with GOD, it's going to involve getting to know Him, not just going to church. Many times people think that just going to church on Sunday is doing God a favor, but it doesn't take a lot of effort to get up and go to church. On the other hand however, to grow, it's going to take us being intentional about a real relationship with God. In order for someone to be passionate about God, He must first, get ahold of your heart. Your heart is what God is really after in the first place. As a matter of fact, it's the one thing He's always been after.

Sometimes we in Christendom, make the mistake of thinking that God is out to hurt us, or to frustrate us, and make our life miserable, but just the contrary he is trying to make us come after Him wholeheartedly. What God really wants is a lifelong loving relationship with his children, and He simply can't have that with weekend visitations only.

GOD WILL BE THERE WHEN OTHERS WALK AWAY

I want to encourage you my friend, who is holding this book in your hand, no matter what type of card life has dealt you, play that hand, but please don't throw in the towel. I can promise you that with God, all things are possible. The Book of Hosea is about the love God have for his people, who chose to love others and turn their backs on him.

There may be some of you who are reading this book who has experience firsthand, how it feels to love someone, and want that person so badly to love you back, but you had to finally face the fact that it takes both parties in the relationship to make it work. Why? Because in any relationship, there are going to be many ups and downs, misunderstandings, and disagreements, breakups and makeups.

WORK IT OUT

But at the end of the day, God simply wants to know, do you love me, do you trust me, do you believe in me, do you want to spend the rest of your life in eternity with me. If the answer is yes, then work through the pain, the adversity, the loneliness, and all the times when it seems like I've left your life, because it's in those time, we are bonding together. It's in those times, if you can wait patiently on me to come in my own timing and not yours, you will see my hand and my provisions in your life.

It is not just a cliché, it's true when they say "love hurts" because it actually does, just ask any married couple who's been married for 5, 10, 15, 20 years, who is willing to be honest with you. They will tell you, as glamorous as our marriage looks right now, if the truth were to be told, along with the PASSION, we share as a married couple, we would not love each other as much, if we did not have the PAIN to go along with it. It is recorded in the Job 2:10, "Should we expect good at the hand of the Lord only, and not evil"..."Pain and Passion" are kin. Every person wants to experience passion in a natural relationship, but have you ever considered this, pain has some good traits as well, because without pain, many times you would never know something is wrong with us. Man this is good stuff.

12

I LOVE MY HUBBY

LADY RITA'S POINT OF VIEW

"Who can find a virtuous woman? For her price is far above rubies. The heart of her husband doth safely trust in her, so that he shall have no need of spoil. She will do him good and not evil all the days of her life", (King James Version, Proverbs 31:10-12)

The film, *Mahogany*, starring Billy D. Williams and Diana Ross is one of my favorite movies of all time. It's so inspiring and it has so many great lines. The storyline, too, is very relevant for couples today. The focus is on two individuals who had nothing when they first met. As they each pursued career opportunities, though, they almost lose each other.

"What good is it for someone to gain the whole world, yet forfeit their soul? Or what can anyone give in exchange for their soul", (New International Version, Mark 8:36-37)

The movie also reminds me of Steve and me. I remember when he proposed like it was yesterday. There we were, back in 1988. He asked me to marry him and was so honest about what our marriage would be.

He said to me, "I have nothing to give you. Nothing except my heart and a beautiful baby girl." (My step-daughter Latasha was four at the time). I didn't hesitate to say yes, though. Nothing about Steve's honesty was scary to me. Nothing about the situation struck me as a problem or a challenge. And it hasn't been. Our marriage has been heaven on earth from the very beginning.

Steve has loved me for me. He's My best friend, my mentor, my teacher. He washes me with the Word of God. He's also my biggest fan, my best supporter. And he's always allowed me to be those things for him. He has never shut me out or excluded me. He has always made sure I am as much a part of his life as he is a part of mine.

He's brought out the best in me, too. He has pushed me, even when I have wanted to give up. He has challenged me, when it's mattered, to dream the dream and be the best I can.

It's not always been easy, though, and we both admit that. The first year of marriage was particularly hard and I think we both wanted a divorce at some point. Most of the problems were material, though. The first house we bought together was roach-infested and we realized that we were expecting our first child about the same time.

Still, even with all of our struggles, the lack of money, something kept me going. Some little voice told me to stick with it, that it wouldn't always be that way. As I think back over our lives, I think about all the trials and how we have come through them. We now have three beautiful children: LaTasha, Steven, and Jamaica. We even have a bonus, my Grammy award, Shekinah.

After the roach-infested home, we moved on and up. We've had three more homes together and one that we built from the ground up. God has allowed us to have a wonderful life together, so wonderful. Our togetherness was so complete.

By now, you can just imagine how I felt when my husband became sick. Of course, I knew something was wrong because his behavior patterns changed and I found him being private. One morning God lead to go and anoint Steve from head to toe and to just pray for strength.

When I approached, though, to pull back the covers, thinking that Steve was still asleep, actually, he grabbed the covers and asked what I was doing. I said, "excuse me," because many times I had prayed and he had done the same thing to me. But then he said, "wait, I need to talk to you. It's nothing to be alarmed about but I have purple like bruises all over. I feel great. I know it's nothing." Well, I made my own assumptions.

It was Sunday morning before church. I knew we had a full day but I was determined to get him to the doctor. In my heart, I thought it was maybe an allergic reaction. I thought they'd probably give him a shot and it would clear right up.

By the end of day, though, we had been to the local doctor's and had gone from nothing to having death, fear, depression, oppression, panic, disbelief, and The Unknown invade our lives.

Satan himself showed up and said to me, "I'm not leaving until I have Steve." He told me, "He's saved. So by dying he would be with Jesus, and what he had was unto death."

But then God spoke up and said, "I've already gone before you and have shown you the result. Remember the Dream!"

As the seasons in our life begin to take on a new face, I fully understood that each season required different needs and the approach demanded God's direction. My husband needed my vows! For BETTER OR WORST, RICHER OR POORER IN SICKNESS AND IN HEALTH!

He needed me to intercede more than he needed me to build his ego. When you are sick or have a sick mate, sex should be last thing on your mind. But it's nothing to be ashamed of. We live real life and you are only as good as your health. Communication is the key. I had to build him up in the Spirit because that was the key to manifestation in his body.

The NASB version of Proverbs 18:14 says, "The SPIRIT of a man can endure his SICKNESS, but as for a broken SPIRIT who can bear it? A lot of what we experience is spiritual and when we are ignorant to Satan's devices, we look to the flesh, which is a trick of the enemy. We wrestle not against flesh and blood.

I heard Donald Lawrence say we are a spiritual being, having an earthly experience. With that being said, you also find out what your marriage is really made of when your earthly experience becomes a real test.

My husband, in his sickness, needed a wife that could get in touch with God in a hurry! He needed to know, at the weakest point in his life, that his wife wouldn't cheat; that taking care of him was not a burden, but a privilege. When the death angel came, trying to get in the hospital door, in the car door, in our house door, the church house door, the chemo room door, and the waiting room door, I stood up through much travail and intercession and told him "THE BLOOD OF JESUS IS AGAINST YOU DEVIL! IT HAS BEEN APPLIED TO THE DOOR POST, DEVIL! YOUR ACCESS IS DENIED!"

Before you let the devil win, fight like a mad girl! I had to know God for myself and I had to know His word. It wasn't a time to use prosperity scripture when my husband needed healing.

My husband's first diagnosis was ITP, a blood disorder that caused him to hemorrhage. The second diagnosis was a mass sitting between his heart and lungs. But God BLOCKED IT!

"Because of the covenant I made with you, sealed with blood, I will free your prisoners from death in a waterless dungeon. Come back to the place of safety, all you prisoners who still have hope! I promise this very day that I will repay two blessings for each of your troubles", (New Living Translation, Zechariah 9:11-12).

I came from Steve's ribs. I was fashioned and designed just for him. I did the work and I understood my place in his life as a helpmeet. When you are a real helpmeet, you live a life of prayer and covering for your family. Steve needed my help and no devil in hell was going to take his health, his vision, his desire!

I realized, too, if I was going to help him, I had to drop all the petty arguments, all the minor disagreements. I had to understand that being right did not matter. Having an ear to hear what the Spirit was saying was a must, crucial to winning the battle.

Many doctors know science, but we know Jesus. We take science facts to the Truth! Jesus told him, "I am the way, the truth, and the life. No one can come to the Father except through me", (John 14:6). We don't have to accept anything that don't line up with what God's Word has already decreed and declared over our lives. So discernment is so crucial. The Holy Ghost will lead you to the right doctors, those who really has your best interest at heart.

There were many days I fasted and prayed, too. We can't ask others to do the work and we not sow toward our own breakthrough! I was determine to seek God on this matter and to follow his every lead even when God was silent saying absolutely nothing. I learned to be still and know He was God.

I recall several instances when a particular doctor came in the room trying to force our hand because of a finding. They would want us to make a decision right then and we said "No!" Then they would try to pressure us and we said "No!"

What the doctor didn't know was that everything he said and every diagnosis, everything, we took to God in prayer. The Holy Ghost would lead us to research the procedure, the side effects, and the risk, which most of the time doctors don't share with patients. The Holy Ghost will tip you off.

"My people are destroyed for lack of knowledge. Because you have rejected knowledge, I also will reject you from being My priest. Since you have forgotten the law of your God, I also will forget your children," (Hosea 4:6)

Have faith in God first, then the doctors, because God is the Healer! "I inquired of the Lord cried out and he heard me and delivered me out of all my troubles", (Psalm 34:4). There's often a process that none of us want to embark upon nor do we feel we are prepared or ready for. I've learn that God is the master teacher and he determines when tests and pop quizzes are given.

Persistence in prayer and bulldog faith in God's Word always produce God's revealed plan! God gave me my Man back, because he still has much work to do! "She openeth her mouth with wisdom; and in her tongue is the law of kindness. She looketh well to the ways of her household, and eateth not the bread of idleness. Her children arise up, and call her blessed; her husband also, and he praiseth her. Many daughters have done virtuously, but thou excellest them all. Favour is deceitful, and beauty is vain: but a woman that feareth the Lord, she shall be praised. Give her of the fruit of her hands; and let her own works praise her in the gates", (King James Version, Proverbs 31:26-31).

13

PRAYER FOR THE SICK

(ALSO AVAILABLE ON CD)

Father, in Jesus's wonderful magnificent name, Lord we thank you. This is the day the Lord has made. We will rejoice and be glad in it. I thank you now God. As we come to pray and call on your name that those who read this book be blessed in their bodies. In their bodies, healing takes place. We thank you Lord. The scriptures say you were wounded for our transgressions. You were bruised for our iniquity, the chastisement of our peace were upon you and with your stripes we are healed. We give your name the praise, the glory and all the honor. Our prayer is for all who read this book be healed by the blood of Jesus. Amen.

Father in the name of Jesus we just come honoring your name. I thank you that you are the God that heal us. I thank you right now; that you have sent your word to heal us by the stripes of Jesus. We are healed. We are made whole. I thank you that nothing is too hard for you God. We give every sickness and disease to you; you were whipped on your back so that we can walk in total healing. So we decree and declare that every person that is reading this book right now is being healed and made whole by the power of the words. By the power of the spoken prayer, by the power and authority of our almighty God. We decree right now speedy healing come forth. Manifest in their bodies, in their souls, their spirit and in their mind. I thank you right now for every negative report being made positive by the power of prayer and intercessors. We count it done. We thank you for the performance. We thank you for the manifestation. God we thank you for the now blessing. We thank you for the good report and we give you glory for it. In Jesus name we pray. Hallelujah, Hallelujah! Amen.

Isaiah 53 says, "who has believed the report of the Lord and to whom has the arm of the Lord been revealed." We come now to thank you Jesus. By the stripes of Jesus you who are reading this book are healed. He took your sickness upon him. He carried your pain. I believe it is the will of God for you to be healed in Jesus's name. Be healed in the name of Jesus. I break every curse of infirmity, every curse of sickness and every curse of premature death off of your body right now in Jesus's name. Glory to God! In the name of Jesus and by the authority of God I break every curse of witchcraft and destruction off your body. From every side of your family, both sides of your family, IT BE BROKEN in Jesus name. The blood of Jesus is applied. In the name of Jesus I speak to every sickness that have invaded your body. I command it by the authority of Jesus to leave now in Jesus name. In the name of Jesus I speak parenthetically to diabetes, to high blood pressure and to cancer. You have to go heart attack, strokes and multiple sclerosis. Be removed and cast into the sea. In Jesus's name, I speak to your hearts, kidneys, lungs, your back, and your liver. Any organ problems be removed and be thou cast into the sea in Jesus's name. I speak to the blood and skeletal system. Bone conditions be removed and be cast into the sea in Jesus name. Hallelujah!

I thank you God that you hear us when we pray and have released healing to your people. "The spirit of the Lord is upon me, because the Lord has anointed me to preach good tidings to the poor. He has sent me to heal the brokenhearted, to comfort all who mourn to give them beauty for ashes. The oil of joy for mourning and the garment of praise for the spirit of heaviness", that "they may be called trees of righteousness, the planting of the Lord that he may be glorified", (Isaiah 61:1, 3). Oh God you "bring health and healing." You "will heal my people and reveal to them their abundance of peace and truth", (Jeremiah 33:6). I quicken the people of God to fear the Lord so the Son of righteousness may arise with healing in its wings", (Malachi 4:2). Just like Jesus, I am released to go "preaching the gospel of the kingdom, and to healing all kinds of disease and sickness" so that the name of the "fame" of Jesus goes throughout the whole world. Let it be that "sick people who are afflicted with various diseases and torments, and those who are demon possessed and paralyzed" come my way that I may heal them in the name of Jesus, (Matthew 4: 23-24). I thank you Lord for your word.

Yes, I speak now to Lupus and every other disease. I command you to leave every sick body now in Jesus's name. Every hidden sickness, every hidden disease I command you to leave their body now in Jesus's name. You are trespassing. Arthritis I speak to you now. Pain, rheumatism I speak to you now. You must go in the name of Jesus. You are trespassing. I command every type of pain to leave their body right now in Jesus name. I come against skin conditions in the name of Jesus. I speak to infections in the body. Come out of their body right now. In Jesus's precious name we pray. I speak to breathing conditions. I speak to asthma, hay fever, sinus, chest congestion and pneumonia. Come out of their body now. In Jesus's name they are healed. They are healed. Joint conditions, pain of the joints, pain in the muscles must go right now in Jesus's name. I come against any conditions and infirmities that may affect this person whether woman or man. Lupus, fibrosis, tumors of the female organs, we speak to them now and command them to leave. In Jesus's name, I come against any kind of sickness that may affect this person as being a man. I speak to every male organ now. I command your organs to function the way God intended for them to function. I command every tumor right now to die and dry up at the roots. I loose the fire of God to burn out every tumor now. In the name of Jesus it must come out. I come against nervous conditions; insomnia that prevents you from sleeping at night, and acid reflux. God has not given you the spirit of fear but of power and of love and a sound mind in Jesus's name. Hallelujah!

Father we agree. We accept the call. I will go and heal those that need healing, (Matthew 8:7). I am "moved with compassion for the sick because they are weary and scattered like sheep have no shepherd", (Matthew 9:36). I will "heal the sick, raise the dead, cleanse the lepers and cast out demons" as freely as I have received I will freely give", (Matthew 10:8). I declare that "the power of God is present to heal" his people, (Luke 5:17). I receive the multitudes. I will "speak to them about the kingdom of God and will heal them" in the name of Jesus, (Luke 9:11). I will "stretch forth" my "hand to heal so that signs and wonders may be done through the name of Jesus", (Acts 4:30). By the word of the lord people are healed, (Psalm 107:20). I will be a faithful ambassador who brings health and healing, (Proverbs 13:17). As the sick are laid at my feet I declare that the healing anointing of Jesus will follow through me and they will be healed, (Matthew 15:30). I will lay hands on the sick so that they may be healed and they will live! They will live! THEY WILL LIVE! (Mark 5:23).

Yes, as you read this book say, "I expect to be healed. I expect to be healed. I expect to live and not die. I expect to recover in the name of Jesus." Right now I speak to heart and circulatory conditions. I speak to irregular heartbeat. I speak to stroke conditions. They must leave your body now. You are the temple of the holy spirit. Every sickness, disease and infirmity must leave your body now. In Jesus's name I speak to digestive disorders and allergies to certain foods that cause you to flare up and be sick. You have no place in the person's body. You must go now in Jesus name. I speak to the spirit of fibromyalgia now, that cause them to live in pain day after day, be healed, be healed in Jesus name. I speak right now to addiction to pain pills. In the name of Jesus, you cannot be bound by the spirit of addiction of any kind. Your body is designed to heal itself and I thank you God, by the blood of Jesus, the addiction is broken off of your body. In Jesus's name I speak to corroded disc in your back, slipped disc, spine conditions, back conditions and neck problems in Jesus's name. By the spirit of the living God, back be aligned right now and be put back into place. In the name of our Lord and Savior Jesus Christ I release miracles right now to take place as you read this book; healing to take place in your body right now. Just declare in the name of Jesus, "I am healed. I am not trying to get healed. I am already healed in Jesus's name".

Father I thank you. I rebuke unclean spirits and sickness in children by the anointing of Jesus Christ. I will heal them and return them to the care of their parents, (Luke 9:42). I may not have silver. I may not have gold, but what I do have I give the anointing to heal those who are sick in the name of Jesus. I speak to those who are ill, rise up and walk, (Acts 3:6-7). I will observe and see that those who came have the faith to be healed. I will call them out right now in their infirmity and say stand straight up on your feet in the name of Jesus. They will manifest healing, (Acts 14:9-10). I will go visit the sick and pray for them. We will lay hands on them and they shall recover and be healed according to Acts 20:8. As the sick are brought before us we agree that they are able by the anointing to be healed by faith. I declare and decree them to be healed and made whole. Your sins have been forgiven according to Matthew 9:2. I declare by this great faith. I thank you that healing is coming forth. In the name of Jesus, overtake them by your healing virtue. We claim it. We decree it. We declare it and it be so says the Lord in Jesus's name. Amen.

In Jesus's name, while you are reading this book, whether in the hospital room, the comforts of your home, nursing home or wherever you are right now agree with us as we pray. I am healed in Jesus name. He was wounded in his body that you might be healed and even as we pray I release miracles of healing to take place in your body now. In Jesus's name the blood of Jesus is applied right now, to every part of your body from head to toe. I believe God for miracles of healing to take place in your life; not only your life, but also in your family member's life, where ever you may go in Jesus's name. Thank you Jesus. Thank you Lord for healing right now. Thank you for delivering, oh God, from all types of sickness, pains and disease. In Jesus's name, Lord we believe it to be done. Lord I speak now to every condition, every sickness, every pain, every doctor's report; I speak to it now. The blood of Jesus is against you Satan. Right now you have been relieved of your assignment against this person. You are trespassing. I am not asking you but, I command you to leave their body in Jesus name.

In Jesus's name, Father we agree with the man of God. Right now we just continue that the healing of the Lord will spring forth speedily, (Isaiah 58:8). "I cry out to you oh God and you healed me. You kept me alive" (Psalm 32:3). By the stripes of Jesus I am healed. " Speak a word Lord and heal me this very hour" (Matthew 8: 8,13). I declare that I am in good health and I am alive, (Genesis 43:28). The "fear of the Lord is health to my body and strength to my bones" (Proverbs 3:7-8). I will give attention to the word of God. I will incline my ear to his sayings. They will not depart from my eyes. I will keep them in the midst of my heart because they are my life and to me health in my body (Proverbs 4:20,22). I will speak with wisdom and promote health (Proverbs 12:18). "I will receive and only speak "pleasant words. They are like a honeycomb; sweetness to my soul and health to my bones" (Proverbs 16:24). I declare that I prosper in all things and I am in good health and the just shall also prosper (John 3:2,3). "As heaven and earth is my witness I choose life so that both my descendants and I will live say the Lord" (Deuteronomy 30:19). I declare oh Lord that you are my life and the length of my days. I love you. I choose to obey you and I cling to you (Deuteronomy 30:20). I declare oh Lord that you are the restorer of life – Hallelujah!- and the nourishment of my old age. You have redeemed my life form the adversary. You do not take away life, but you give life and I thank you right now that life is coming forth against every doctor's report. I speak life God. Whose report shall we believe? We shall believe the report of the Lord and the report of the Lord says I am healed. I am whole and I give you praise right now in the name of Jesus. I lay hands on my own body and I decree the manifold healing of Jesus. In the name of Jesus, right there where you are, if you on your sofa, if you are laying in your bed, if you in the bathroom, if you are standing in the kitchen, lay hands on your body and say by the stripes of Jesus I decree and declare healing come forth now in the name of Jesus. And it is so Hallelujah!

I speak right now to miracle healing. I thank you that signs and wonders manifest according to the word of God, which is infallible, it cannot fail. Be released right now in Jesus name. The devil is a liar. You will not be depressed. You will not be oppressed. You will not be suppressed. That spirit be broken right now off your life. Rise up! Open up those windows; open up those blinds and let the sunlight come in. This darkness is not of God and I thank you right now. As you begin to open your eyes and speak with faith that I am healed. I shall live and declare the works of the Lord. The spirit of the living God will begin to move mightily and expeditiously on your behalf. Be released from this spirit right now of infirmity in Jesus name. I thank you Lord that healing is coming forth and is coming forth right now. I pray with you now, Lord forgive us for allowing fear and guilt and self-rejection, even self-hatred, sometimes forgiveness, bitterness, sin or even pride or rebellion to open the door for any sickness or infirmity to invade my body. I renounce them now and I am free – Hallelujah! - of this spirit now in Jesus's name. Jesus carried all my sickness according to Matthew 8:17. I don't have to carry it. He carried it for me and for you. In Jesus's name, I break right now the spirit of cancer. I cast out the spirit of cancer. You are a lying devil you spirit of cancer. We speak to you now, as you come right now and try to establish yourself upon this individuals lungs, upon their bones, upon their breast, upon their throat, their back, their spine, their liver, their kidneys, their pancreas, skin, legs or stomach. In the name of Jesus, spirit of cancer I curse you now at the root. They will live and not die. They shall declare the works of the lord in Jesus name.

Father God, in the name of Jesus, I take authority over every person 's mind who is reading this book right now. I come against every spirit of oppression and depression and I cast it back to the pits of hell from which it came. Lord I thank you. Lord you have not given them a spirit of fear; but, I thank you right now that they have a sound mind. I thank you right now in the name of Jesus Lord your peace is coming to them. Reassurance that God's word is forever settled in heaven. I thank you Lord that you have the final say. Lord we thank you right now in the name of Jesus that the peace of God is coming in their room right now. Where there has been depression and oppression God's peace resides. Lord, where they have been thinking they were going to die and not make it through the night I speak life. God I thank you right now that ministering angels are encamped about their bedside. God begin to minister to them. Lord I thank you for the healing virtue of Jesus Christ right now. No devil in hell can stand against the righteous Lord. We apply the blood. The blood of Jesus is applied to the door post of this house right now God. We fortify this house God through intercession. God by your word we say live and not die. Declare the works of the Lord in the name of Jesus. We thank you right now for such an awesome testimony that's coming forth. Begin to say with me I am healed. I am healed. I feel healed. I speak healed. I declare healed. In the name of Jesus restoration to their bodies. Now God we touch and agree in the name of Jesus that restoration of all things are coming back to them. Finances, even regarding their sickness. God where they have gone through and bills have piled up, we speak a breakthrough of prosperity in the name of Jesus to come forth. God in their house peace. Peace. Peace be still in this home. In the name of Jesus we declare and decree it. Now God we declare healing in their marriage. God we declare healing with their children. God we declare healing everywhere they hurt. God you are the God that heals. We touch and agree by faith that the power of God is breaking forth and taking place in their homes. In the name of Jesus, live my daughter, live my son. Live now says the Lord in the name of Jesus.

You can trust the Lord. If you are reading this book know that you can trust the Lord. I know your body is in pain. I know you are feeling the effects of it; nevertheless you can trust the Lord. You can trust the Lord because of his word. Psalm 91 says, "He who dwells in the shelters of the most high will abide under the shadow of the Almighty. I will say to the Lord, my refuge and fortress, my God, in whom I trust. For it is He who delivers me from the snare of the trapper and from the deadly pestilence. He will cover me with feathers and under his wings I can find refuge. His faithfulness is a shield and buckler. You will not be afraid of the terror by night or the arrow that flies by day of the pestilence that stalks in darkness or the destruction that lays waste at noon day a thousand may fall at your side, ten thousand - Glory to God! – "may fall at your right hand but it shall not approach you" according to the word of the living God. "You will only look on with your eyes and see the recompense of the wicked for you have made the lord your refuge, even the most high your dwelling place. No evil shall befall you nor any plague come near your tent. For he will give his angels charge concerning you my son, my daughter, to guard you in all your ways. They will lift you up in their hands least you strike your foot against a stone. You will tread upon the lion and the cobra. The young lion and the serpent you will trample down because you have loved the Lord, therefore he will deliver you. I will set him securely on high because he's known my name. He will call upon me and I will answer him. I will be with him in trouble saith the Lord. I will rescue him or her that honors me with long life." I want to say that again. As you read this book, the word of God says "with long life." Psalm 91:16 says: "with long life I will satisfy you and let him behold my salvation."

Yes Father right now while your daughter and your son is sitting there crying, while their body is wrecking with pain, I thank you right now that the reality of you being there with them is more real than any pain or any fear they feel right now. I ask right now for you Lord to wrap your arms around them. Now put your arms around yourself as if Jesus is sitting there and embrace yourself with the love of God; because right now I'm telling you in this very moment He is there with you and He wants to love you. He wants to minister to you through this which you are going through. Know that you are not alone. The tears are real, but you are not alone. God is ever with you. He's a very present help in time of trouble. He is a very present help when you have received a negative report. He is a very present help when you see no way out. God is near. He is present and He loves you daughter. He loves you in the name of Jesus. Be blessed. Be encouraged. Be strengthened. Know that your God is faithful and He is not a man that he shall lie. That every promise he has spoken to you is "yes" and "amen". Hallelujah!

In Jesus's name, I want you to know that he loves you so much that he died for you. He took all of your sickness upon himself. I want you to know as you read this book, as we come to the close of it, I want you to know he went by the whipping post and He stayed there. They tied my Lord and your Lord to the whipping post and He took 39 stripes in his body for you and for I. They cut his back open. They cut his flesh open. Every stripe that He took in his back was so that you could receive a healing in your body. I want you to stand, declare and decree, that according to the word of God you are healed. I know you have the doctor's report and it is real. You feel the pain in your body and it's real. I want you to stand up and declare that you are healed by the blood of Jesus.

Maybe you are sitting there and you are walking in un-forgiveness or something is in your heart that may have held up your healing. I ask you right now to say these words: Father God, reveal to me what I don't know that may be present in my heart; or someone in my heart I have not forgiven. I ask you right now give me the authority and power by almighty God to forgive them and release them. That my healing may come forth. I receive it now. I choose to forgive and walk in love. It doesn't matter what has been done to me I love God; therefore, I love the brethren and I forgive in Jesus's name, Amen.

In case you're not saved as you read this book, I want you to repeat these words and invite Jesus to come into your life:

Dear God, I am a sinner and I believe that Jesus Christ is the son of God and I believe that Jesus died for all of my sins and I believe that he was buried for all of my sins. I also believe that God the Father raised Jesus out of the grave that I might be saved now. Today I am saved. Thank you Jesus. I am saved. Hallelujah! Glory to God! In Jesus's name. Amen.

Be healed my daughter. Be healed my son in Jesus name. We love you. We are praying for you. From New Destiny Christian Church and the bottom of our hearts we love you. Remember somebody loves you and someone is praying for you in Jesus's name. Amen.

Tell everybody about the goodness of Jesus. Share your testimony that Jesus still heals in Jesus's name. Amen.

Works Cited

www.americanpregnancy.org/gettingpregnant/understandingovulation.html

www.livesciencecom/37022-speed-of-sound-mach-1.html

www.wisegeek.org/what-is-the-speed-of-sound.html

www.freedictionary.com/molecule

www.biography.com

www.leaderu.com/orgs/tul/psychtoday9809/html

www.largestfastestsmartest.co.uk/animals-with-the-best-sense-of-hearin-in-the-world/

Maldonado, Guillermo. The Glory of God. Pennsylvania: Whitaker House, 2012.

Heflin, Ruth Ward. Glory. Maryland: McDougal Publishing, 1990.

Herzog, David. Glory Invasion. Pennsylvania: Destiny Images, 2012.

Ellis, Neil C. Pursuing the Glory. Pennsylvania: Spirit Publishers, 2010.

Vernon, R. A. Dr. Size Does Matter. Ohio: Victory Media Publishing Company, 2011.

ABOUT THE AUTHOR

Pastor Steve Smith is the founder and senior pastor of New Destiny Christian Church, Gadsden, AL. He is honored to be married to the very lovely Lady Rita Smith. They have three beautiful children.

www.ingramcontent.com/pod-product-compliance
Lightning Source LLC
Chambersburg PA
CBHW070828250626
47170CB00006B/2248